W9-BMG-202

WITHDRAWN

AN AVALON ROMANCE

A NEW BEGINNING
Debby Mayne

When Bethany Moore returns to her childhood home she is heartbroken to find that the old oak tree behind the house is gone.

Reverend David Hadaway, the new owner of the house, makes no apologies for cutting down the tree because it was threatening the foundation.

Along with the loss of the house, the tree, and her grandmother's failing health, Bethany's world has been shaken to its core. But with David's patience and steadfast commitment to always doing the right thing, she realizes what's really important in life.

It finally takes being forced to make a major, life-altering decision before she can act on her heart's desires and accept true love.

A NEW
BEGINNING

•

Debby Mayne

AVALON BOOKS
NEW YORK

PRINTED IN THE UNITED STATES OF AMERICA
ON ACID-FREE PAPER
BY HADDON CRAFTSMEN, BLOOMSBURG, PENNSYLVANIA

This book is dedicated to my mother-in-law, Bobbie Mayne,
and my dad's wife, Eileen Fish Tisdale,
two very remarkable women.

I'd like to thank friends Denise Camp, Kathy Carmichael, Connie Keenan, and Kimberly Llewellyn for their ongoing support and encouragement. And the wonderful people who work at the Oldsmar post office have been some of the best cheerleaders a writer could ask for.

Chapter One

The cloudless sky hung overhead like a shroud above the small town of Clearview. Robins sang and an occasional cardinal stood on the branches of trees that had mostly lost their leaves, leaving a blanket of color on the ground. A light breeze lifted the autumn air still tinged with the spirit of summer. Bethany remembered her grandfather saying that the weatherman couldn't make up his mind on days like this, so he gave them the best of both summer and autumn. She had to lean against the rental car to keep her balance as the memories flooded her mind and soul. The pain was like the air—hints of days past mixed with the mystery of what lay ahead. She shuddered.

Bethany squinted her eyes as she stood at the opening of the tree-lined cul-de-sac where her grandmother used to live. If she cocked her head to one side and looked through the slits of narrowed eyes, she could still see how things used to be.

All kinds of feelings washed over her—a blend of

1

happiness and regret, nostalgia and remorse, warmth and pain. If she closed her eyes and listened really closely, she could almost hear her mother calling her name to come in for dinner.

Bethany's grandmother, the woman she'd called Nana, had lived in that house since a few years after her marriage to Grandpa, who died when Bethany was still a teenager. After her parents' divorce, Bethany and her mother moved in with the understanding that it was only a temporary arrangement. Physically, it was, but emotionally, Bethany still felt attached to the big, two-story colonial house that sat perched at the end of the street. It was still there, but it was different.

She parallel parked her rental car halfway down the street so she could experience one of the joys of her youth—seeing her lighthouse at the end of the street as she approached home. The feeling in the pit of her stomach was from a longing for the way things used to be.

The house was still painted gray, and the wrap-around porch looked the same; but still, there was something different. Bethany took slow, deliberate steps forward, and as she approached, she continued squinting her eyes, trying to figure out what had changed.

By the time she reached her grandmother's old yard, she still hadn't figured it out. She just stood there and openly stared at the structure, allowing her heart to take over and guide her through myriad emotions that she couldn't explain to herself in her own thoughts. So she allowed herself to quit thinking and just feel.

Bethany took a deep breath, allowing the crispness of the early fall day to enter her nostrils. Jasmine was still in bloom, and she felt herself drift to another time—a time when things were simple and decisions were made for her.

Sure, it hurt when her parents split up, but coming to live with Nana was the second best thing for her. Her mother said that she wanted Bethany to experience some of the same joys she'd had growing up. And she had. Unfortunately, she hadn't seen or heard from her father since her parents' divorce, but the adults who were still in her life did everything they could to make up for it.

She'd been safe and loved in this wonderful old house where she was free to explore every nook and cranny. Her grandmother encouraged her to enjoy the outdoors, and she'd taught her to plant flowers. They'd even had a small vegetable garden out back until the oak tree had grown so big that it cast too much shade over the backyard for vegetables to grow.

That was it! The oak tree was gone! She knew something was missing.

Bethany's heart pounded as she ran around behind the house, not even thinking that she didn't have the right to be there on someone else's property. This was Nana's house, and it always would be.

There, in the place where the massive oak tree once was, stood a tiny sapling that looked like it had just been planted. Tears immediately sprang to her eyes. The oak tree was gone, and that meant that a little piece of her heart had been chipped away as well. She loved that tree.

Suddenly, the back screen door flew open, and a small boy ran out. When he spotted Bethany, he froze. In spite of her recent emotional upheaval, she allowed her lips to tweak into a slight smile. He just stood there and stared for a moment before running back into the house, yelling, "Uncle Dave, there's a lady outside in our backyard."

"Who is she?" a male voice said.

"I don't know. Just some lady," the high-pitched voice answered.

Bethany took a few steps back toward the front of the house. She was afraid she'd made a huge mistake in coming back. Someone else lived in Nana's old house. What right did she have to walk around, acting like she owned the place?

Just then, a male figure appeared in the doorway. She couldn't make out his features because of the shadows from the house. "Are you looking for someone?" he said.

Bethany opened her mouth to speak, but words wouldn't come out. The little boy darted past the man, saving her from having to say anything for a moment and allowing her to catch her breath. She hadn't planned to talk to anyone; she only wanted to look and let the memories drift through her mind.

"Well?" the man said, taking a step outside and letting the screen door slam behind him. She winced. Nana would have fussed at him about that.

Bethany noticed the firmness of his jaw line, and her heart skipped a beat as her mouth flew open. Just because he was so masculine looking didn't mean she could stand there and gawk at him, so she clamped her teeth together.

"I-I just wanted to see this house. My grandmother lived here, and I . . . uh, I lived here for a few years when I was little. My name is Bethany Moore."

Bethany found herself stuttering and shifting her weight from foot to foot, not knowing what to do with her hands. The man's face softened, and a smile slowly crept across it. He closed the gap between them and extended his hand.

"I'm David Hadaway, and I bought this old house last year. Gertie Chalmers is your grandmother, right?"

Bethany nodded. "She just went into a nursing home."

David Hadaway frowned. "Yes, I'm aware of that. When she sold me this house, she told me that she was moving to a retirement center. Too much yard work here, she said." He looked at Bethany and hesitated for a moment before asking, "I just saw her last week. How is she?"

"I'm not sure yet. I just got into town." Bethany watched the man and tried very hard to dislike him, but she couldn't. In spite of the fact that he lived in her grandmother's house, she couldn't help but notice his kind eyes and genuine concern.

He let out a hefty sigh and said, "That's good." He looked over at the little boy and said, "Pick up your toys, Jonathan."

"Does he live here with you?" Bethany asked, not able to hold back her curiosity.

David nodded. "Right now, he does. At least, until my brother and his wife get things straight between them." He looked away from Bethany and then zoomed his focus back on her, weakening her knees. "Would you like to come inside and take a look around? I don't mind."

"You don't?" Bethany asked, not knowing what she should do.

She'd only come to let some of her warm childhood memories comfort her, but she didn't expect to be allowed inside. She was willing to settle for a look around the yard and to stare at the house for a few minutes. "Are you sure?"

"I'm sure," he said, taking a step back and holding the door open for her. "C'mon in."

She slowly took a step into the kitchen that had once been her refuge from the outside world. Whenever life got her down, she knew that she could always count on Nana to bake a batch of cookies, and together, they'd sit at the huge kitchen table and talk things over. At least, until her mom came in. The mood always changed then. It became quiet, somber, and sometimes bitter.

Basically, the kitchen looked the same, with the exception of a few changes that didn't really matter. Of course, a different table held the place of honor in the middle of the floor, and there were different appliances sitting out on the countertops.

Bethany turned to him and said, "Does your wife like to cook?"

Shaking his head, he replied, "I don't have a wife, but I enjoy cooking."

"Oh. Sorry." Bethany turned away from David so he wouldn't see her embarrassment.

The little boy ran back inside and said, "All finished, Uncle Dave. I put all my toys away just like you told me to. May I have a cookie now?"

"Excuse me for a minute," David said as he turned and pulled a jar from one of the cupboards. He reached inside and pulled out a huge cookie with white icing. "Here ya go, Jonathan. Don't run with it," he added, causing the child to slow down as he went back outside, the cookie already half gone. David chuckled and looked back at Bethany. "I wish I had that kind of energy."

"Did you buy this house for yourself?" Bethany asked. She knew that she was being nosy, but she wanted to know who'd taken over the place that held so many memories of her past.

"Yes, I did. I know it's too big for one person, but I have a hope to eventually meet the right woman who will help me fill it with lots of children. One of the reasons I bought the house is so that I can stay busy with projects."

"What kind of projects?" Bethany asked, as she cocked her head to one side.

He shrugged. "All sorts of things, really. I enjoy fixing things, renovating rooms, and building furniture." He pointed to a wooden rocking chair in the corner of the huge country-style kitchen. "See that chair over there? That is my latest creation. It took me three months to design and make that. I'm slow, but that's what I like to do in my spare time."

Bethany stood up and walked over to the chair. "It's beautiful," she said, rubbing the back of it and feeling all the intricate etchings that created a floral pattern across the back and down the sides. "You're very talented."

He blushed. "Thank you." He turned away from her, picked up a kettle, filled it with water, and set it on the stove. "I'm making tea. I hope you'll join me." He didn't ask her, but she liked the way he gently but firmly told her what he was about to do.

David busied himself with getting tea bags from the pantry, filling the sugar bowl, cutting lemons, and when the water began to boil, pouring it into the cups. He crossed the room and sat down, placing the tray on the table in the same motion. He gestured with a sweeping motion over the cups. "Help yourself. I tend to be very informal around here. Ever since I moved in, it seems like I've had a steady stream of visitors."

"Relatives?" Bethany asked. She looked out the back window at the little boy who rode his bicycle around in circles on the driveway that circled to the garage.

He nodded. "Some relatives, but mostly members of my congregation."

"Your congregation?" she asked, pausing, holding her cup an inch from her lips.

"Yes," he said, nodding. "I'm the pastor of New Hope, a small nondenominational church about a mile from here."

"But I thought that pastors lived in parsonages provided by the congregation. Why did you buy my grandmother's house?"

He scooped sugar and dumped it into his tea with a quick, firm movement. He glanced up quickly and smiled at her, catching her in the act of staring. Her face became hot. "It's a very small church, and they couldn't afford a house for me yet, so when I took the job, I agreed that I'd use my own savings to purchase this place. It's great because I can help out members of the congregation who need a place to stay for whatever reason." David held out one of his open hands. Bethany noticed that his hands were big and callused.

That revelation made it all the more difficult for Bethany to do what she felt compelled to do. She had to find out why he'd taken down the oak tree that had meant so much to her as a child. She chewed on her bottom lip and looked down at the tabletop.

"Is something bothering you?" he asked. "You look worried."

She shook her head and stared at the table before looking up and into the kindest eyes she'd ever seen. "What did you do with Nana's oak tree?"

"Her oak tree?" he asked, the smile on his face fading.

"Yeah, her oak tree. The one out back."

In spite of her polite upbringing, Bethany heard the bitterness in her words, almost in the same voice she heard when her mother spoke. An eerie feeling washed over her. Still, she couldn't keep the accusatory tone from her voice. She wanted to know what he'd done with the tree that had meant so much to her as she was growing up. It had become a symbol of life to her, and now that she was here, she wanted to see the leaves that turned a deep shade of gold before falling to the ground.

"I had to take it down," he said. He lifted the cup to his lips and took a sip, never taking his eyes off her, making her squirm. He had the amazing ability to bring her stomach to a rumbling roll with just a glance. It was almost as if he could see through to her soul, something she didn't want anyone to do.

"But why?"

He leaned back in his chair and studied her for a moment before answering. "It had grown way too big to be that close to the house."

"You could have trimmed it," she said, her voice cracking. She really loved that oak tree, especially now that it was gone.

"I did, but the roots were already in the sewer system. It had to go." His pleasant expression became guarded. Bethany knew that she'd caused that to happen, and it was really none of her business. This man could do whatever he wanted with the house and yard. He'd bought it from her grandmother who obviously trusted him with the place in which she'd lived most of her life.

"My grandfather planted it." Bethany had no desire for the tea in front of her, and she felt like jumping up and bolting from the room. But she didn't.

"I'm sorry," he said softly as he looked down. Both of his hands rested on the table. Bethany noticed his muscular forearms from under his sleeves that were rolled up to his elbow. They looked rock solid. But she had to take her mind off the man and concentrate on what he'd done to her tree.

"I don't believe you. If you were really sorry, you wouldn't have cut that tree down to begin with. If you were really sorry, it would still be there like it always was when I was a little girl." Bethany couldn't help the fact that she came out sounding like a spoiled little girl now. She had to bite her lip to quit talking so much.

Shaking his head, he said, "It was a beautiful tree—I agree. However, when your grandfather planted it, he didn't take into account the fact that the roots would reach out and take over the entire backyard, making a mess of the sewer and water pipes, not to mention the foundation of the house."

Bethany's eyes began to mist with tears as she felt her chin quiver. "I loved that tree."

David reached out and took her hand from across the table. "I can see that, Bethany. I understand. But there was nothing I could have done to save the tree and the house too. I tried everything I could to have the pipes rerouted, but the master root was getting dangerously close to the foundation of this house, and I didn't want to lose it. So I did the only thing I could."

Bethany looked down at the table and said, "What else have you done to Nana's house?" There it was again, that bitterness, that whiny voice that once belonged to her mother. She bit her lip again.

David stood up and held the chair for her. "Why don't you take a look around? I'll stay here and let you look at your leisure. I'm sure you have a lot of memories you'd like to be alone with."

She nodded as she stood up, her bottom lip still between her teeth. He began clearing the table as she left the kitchen, and she could hear the sounds of cups, saucers, and spoons being washed. As much as she wanted to dislike this man for taking out Nana's tree, she couldn't. He was kind and gentle—just like her grandfather had been, from what she could remember. But still, that oak tree held a special place in her heart. It signified permanence to Bethany, and she wanted it right where it had always been. As Bethany walked through the downstairs part of the house, she saw that it was pretty much as it was when Nana had it, only it used to seem much bigger. In spite of the gnawing nostalgia in the pit of her stomach, she marveled at how things always seemed bigger when she was younger.

The hardwood floors had been cared for, and she would have been hard pressed to find a single large scratch on them. Oriental rugs were scattered about in the high traffic areas and in the center of furniture groupings in the living room, dining room, and den. David was either a neat freak or he had a housekeeper. When she got to the stairs, she slowly climbed them, hopping on the fourth step from the landing. No sound. She jumped again. Silence.

The creak in the boards had been fixed. She had always been able to hear when someone was coming up the stairs as she lay in her bed at night, and it gave her a comforting feeling to know that no one could get past the bottom half dozen steps without making a sound. David had obviously taken care of that. She had no idea why that bothered her, but it did. Just like everything else that wasn't exactly the same.

The chandelier at the top of the landing was sparkling clean, all the prisms casting their own little rainbows on the white wall. That had always lifted her heart, knowing that her life was filled with rainbows, even if they did come from an interior light. At least, that was still the same.

As Bethany opened each bedroom door, she glanced in and found everything exactly like it was before. A four-poster bed stood in the center of the bedroom where

Nana had slept. It didn't look to Bethany like this was David's room. Most of his personal belongings were in the room at the other end of the hall—the room that once belonged to Bethany's mother.

After each door had been opened and each room inspected, Bethany leaned against the wall and shut her eyes. This whole trip was wreaking havoc on her emotions, and she felt like sitting down right where she was for a good cry. Over the past year, her grandmother had sold her house and moved into a retirement home. Since Bethany's mother had died, it was her duty to come and be with Nana since she'd suffered a stroke, so she had to quit her job.

David was being considerate and allowing her to roam freely around his house, and she was taking advantage of it. She didn't want to be rude, but she ached for the familiar sight of that oak tree that had brought her so much comfort and pleasure. There was something about its massive presence that made her feel safe, like nothing could ever really change in her life. But now that tree was gone, and she had more changes than she'd ever imagined.

She sighed and pulled herself away from the wall. It was time to go back downstairs. Bethany knew she needed to straighten up and force herself to thank David for allowing her to look around. It was much more than she'd expected when she decided to visit the old house. As much frustration as she felt in her heart about everything not being exactly the same, in her mind, she knew better than to be rude. After all, no matter how many changes he'd made, none of it was directed at her. He had a right to do whatever he wanted to do, now that this was his house.

When Bethany got to the bottom two steps, she did

another little bounce, trying with all her might to get a sound, but to no avail. Silence prevailed.

"I fixed that," a man's voice said from the other side of the foyer.

Bethany jerked her head up and found herself once again face to face with David Hadaway. She took a deep breath and slowly let it out. "I used to pretend that this was our secret alarm system. It made me feel safe."

He chuckled. "It was an alarm system, all right, but I don't know how secret it was. Those creaks could be heard from practically any room in the house."

"I liked the sound," she said as she set her jaw and looked him squarely in the eye. The stubborn streak her mother said she was born with had returned, and she couldn't seem to hold it back. David just kept on being patient with her, like he probably was with his nephew.

He fixed his gaze on hers and held steady for a few seconds before he offered his arm and said, "Why don't we go out back, and I can show you the tree I planted in place of the oak."

Ignoring the offer of his arm, she followed him and said, "You planted a replacement tree? I saw a twig. Surely, you can't be talking about that." Bethany cut herself off before she said something she might regret. She took a deep breath. "Aren't you afraid the same thing will happen?" Bethany wasn't about to let herself get too close to this man. His charisma and charm weren't lost on her. She felt like she might put herself at too much risk of feeling something she wasn't ready for.

When they reached the back of the house, he held the door for her. She went down the concrete steps her grandfather had lovingly placed and to the edge of the property where a lonely little tree with no leaves stood.

As she got closer, she saw the small tender sapling that had already begun to go through the natural cycle of losing its leaves. Tiny green buds were forming on the tips of the pencil-thin branches. The last traces of summer had fooled the tree into getting ready for spring. Even Bethany knew it would lose the new growth the next time a frost hit.

"This is what you replaced the oak tree with?" Bethany asked as she pointed to the tree. How could he think that something so scrawny could even come close to replacing that majestic oak?

"Yep. That's a tulip poplar." He touched one of the lower branches lovingly as she walked around it.

"But it's so scrawny. I hardly see how it'll ever be as huge as the mighty oak tree that was there," she continued. "In my opinion, it's a poor substitute." She glared at David as his face tightened. He stuck his hand into his pocket. His head nodded as he glanced back and forth between Bethany and the tree.

Finally, he took a deep breath and spoke with gentleness in his voice. "Bethany, anything's a poor substitute for the family you once had."

Chapter Two

Bethany stood there, stunned speechless, and he continued. "I bought this house because I saw that it had a tremendous amount of potential and that it had been lovingly cared for all the years your grandmother had it. However, once I moved in, I realized that some of the things you seem to hold so dear to your heart were the very things that had become problems and the reason your grandmother had to sell it." She had to strain to hear him, his voice was so soft.

Bethany gulped as she watched him move with ease across the yard. She followed, still not talking but listening to David, hoping to find something to trip him up. The smells of late summer still lingered in the air, and there was a slight feeling that autumn had barely begun. Her heart twisted with the memories of her childhood in this very same yard. She remembered jumping into piles of leaves shed by the old oak tree. How long would it be before this new sapling would provide the same amount of autumn leaves? And would they be as pretty as the ones on the oak tree?

"Before we closed on the deal, she revealed all her plumbing bills that had forced her to get rid of the place. Plus, she told me that she needed to make some repairs to the inside, but she was getting too far along in age to have to worry about things like that any more. I took this place off her hands, knowing that it would be a challenge, but that was okay. I have the time and the ability to do most of the work myself, and what I can't do, I can call someone from the church to help. In spite of the fact that we're small, we have quite a bit of talent there."

"But the tree—" Bethany began.

"Yes, the tree," he interrupted. "That was a beautiful old oak tree; magnificent in every season, but not very practical to have right next to the house. I survived the broken windows from the branches that had reached out far beyond anyone ever dreamed and I survived having to reroute the plumbing system. However, when I discovered the roots trying to lift the foundation of the house, I had to do something. But first, I want you to know that I called your grandmother."

"You called Nana?" Bethany asked. "But why? The house is yours. You can do anything you want."

He nodded. "Yes, that's true, but I knew that there had to be a reason she hadn't gotten rid of the tree, even though it was obviously causing problems with the house. I had to find out why."

"What did she say?" Bethany asked, curious as to what that tree meant to Nana.

"She told me that it had been planted a week after she and your grandfather brought your mother home from the hospital. Your mother used to climb it when she was a girl, and you loved to swing under it when you and your mom came to live here. Yes, your grandmother had some very fond memories of that tree."

"And you chopped it down," she stated, her voice falling off in a crackle.

He looked at her, and she felt her heart twisting in a tangle of betrayal. Bethany was now immensely attracted to David, but she didn't want to be. He was the bad guy—the man who tore down her memories and hope for the future. What if she had children of her own someday, and they wanted to climb the tree? That was the only part of her childhood she ever thought she'd be able to share with them, and now it was gone. Bethany had nothing left in her life but the feeling of abandonment. She knew that it reached much deeper than the tree, but that was the only tangible thing she could deal with at the moment—that and all the other changes to the house. He could call it repairs all day long, but it really wasn't necessary as far as she was concerned.

"Yes, I did. But I just showed you that new tree I planted. The tulip poplar is one of the fastest growing trees there is, and I hope to have half my yard shaded within a few years."

"But it's not my tree," she said.

"No," he replied, "It's *my* tree." His voice held a note of finality, and he clamped his jaw shut.

She gasped. David's comment had caught her totally by surprise, and when she tilted her head to look at him from a different angle, he slowly smiled at her warmly.

David scratched his head as he thought about what must be going on in Bethany's mind. Obviously, she'd been hurt pretty badly, so he knew that he had to handle her with kid gloves. The issues she was having to deal with were much greater than an old oak tree.

"Bethany, not everything is going to happen the way I think it should. There are plenty of things I could get angry about or worry over, but when these events happen, I try to sit back and look at the big picture."

Bethany shut her eyes tightly. She looked like she was feeling pain, and she didn't want to see it. As much as David hated inflicting pain on anyone, he knew that there were some things he had to say, so he continued.

"When I first looked at this house, what I saw was a structure that was very pretty. It had obviously been taken care of to the owner's best ability, and a lot of love was poured into it. However, once I got into it and things began to break and fall apart, I found myself wondering if it was worth it. Then, after I took care of the immediate problems, I took a step back and saw it from a different angle. Sure, this house is old, so I couldn't expect it to be like brand new. Even the hidden plumbing problems were something that could be fixed. So I just dove right in and did what had to be done." He made a sweeping gesture with his hands. "And now I have the house just like I want it. Are there still a few little quirks here and there?" He studied her face now that she was looking at him again before answering his own question. "Sure, there are. But I just take care of them, one at a time."

He watched Bethany as she shifted position. It appeared that she'd been really listening to him, but he still wasn't sure. She was pretty angry about that tree when he first started talking to her, and that was an obstacle that he didn't expect to overcome at the first meeting.

"You make it all sound so easy," she said, her face filled with pain.

"No, it's not easy because there are so many hurdles

to get over in life. I know how difficult it is for you to come back here and see all these changes, but I want you to know that I did everything I could to keep things as they were. Your grandmother is a wonderful woman, and she told me that there were problems with the house before she sold it to me."

"She did?" Bethany asked. Her expression nearly broke his heart in two, but he had to remain strong. Hopefully, he'd say and do the right things. David knew that this was one of those times he'd have to rely on his faith to get him through.

"Yes, she did. But I could tell that she still hesitated selling it. That was what made me want to take care of the problems and bring back the beauty of the house. She even gave me a few snapshots of her favorite rooms, as well as the yard. My goal is to have this place in total working order and bring her back to see it."

Bethany's head shot up, and she stared at David. "You'd do that for her?" Her voice was soft, and it bore a hole through to his heart. She was so precious, the last thing he wanted to do was hurt her more than she'd been hurt in her life.

He nodded. "I really like your grandmother. She's a loving woman who has wonderful memories of her family. I even remember her telling me about a granddaughter who brought her so much joy. Is that you?"

Bethany nodded and smiled, in spite of her feelings. He could tell that he'd just brought back a wonderful memory. "I'd like to think so."

He smiled, and Bethany felt her heart begin to thaw as he spoke. "She knew how to make you feel warm and cozy while you brought her pleasure. Sounds like you have a wonderful grandmother."

"I do." Bethany had a hard time staying mad at David.

"Did I tell you that your grandmother has visited me several times since I bought her house?" he asked as they walked back toward the house.

"No, but I figured she would. She really loved this place." The constriction in Bethany's throat was beginning to loosen.

"Yes, she did. When I told her that I needed to remove the oak tree, she came over and looked at it one more time. I saw the sadness on her face, but she knew that I had to take it out. She's a very reasonable woman." His gaze met hers, and a warmth came over her that gave her a little bit more comfort. "I hope you understand."

Shrugging, Bethany looked him in the eye. "Does it really matter whether I understand or not?"

Nodding slowly, she saw that he spoke of nothing but what was honest. "Yes, it matters a great deal." Her stomach felt a giant thud, as if someone had kicked her. She had to take a quick step back to keep her footing. She needed to change the subject. It was getting way too personal.

Bethany averted her gaze and looked around the yard. "I always loved autumn around here." She pointed to the other side of the yard. "I used to have a butterfly garden over there."

He nodded. "Yes, your grandmother told me. I even have a picture of it. I was thinking about doing the same thing for Jonathan since it looks like he might be here for a while."

Bethany spun around. She'd almost forgotten about the little boy. She saw him bicycling around in circles on the driveway. She used to do the same thing when she was a child. "He'll love it," she said. "But do you think he'll still be around in the spring?"

David thrust his hands in his pockets as he turned and looked at Bethany for a moment. The silence was comfortable, and he didn't seem to mind when no one was talking. And when he spoke, he did it in a soft voice. "I'm not sure. It all depends on how long it takes my brother to work through his marital problems." Then, his eyes lit up. "Would you like to come over and help us start planting it next spring? After all, you're the one with the experience."

Bethany laughed nervously. "Oh, I couldn't. I'm sure I'll be long gone by then."

"Now that you're back, why would you want to leave?" he asked as his eyes met hers once again, causing a lump to form in her throat. He had a way of doing that to her, even though they'd just met. She felt like kicking herself.

"There's no reason to stay," she finally managed to say.

"But if I can show you a reason, would you consider it?" His gaze bore through to her soul, and for the first time, she saw a flicker of a different kind in his eyes

"Uh, I'm not sure," she finally managed to say. "I don't even have a job yet."

David shifted his weight from one foot to the other as he looked off in the distance. Then, he looked back at her. "We have several people in our church who are in positions of being able to hire personnel for their companies. Maybe you can talk to them."

"I don't know," Bethany said. "I wouldn't want to take advantage of anyone just to get a job."

David chuckled. "I'm not exactly talking about corporate networking. Just come to church and get to know a few people. We're a loving bunch of people who like to help our own."

With a deep sigh, Bethany nodded as she backed away from David. "I'm sure you are."

He followed her to her rental car, and as she got in, he lifted his hand and wiggled his fingers. "Tell your grandmother I said hello, and I hope she feels better soon. I'm really looking forward to having her over once she's able."

She started the car and drove around the cul-de-sac to leave. As she looked in her rear-view mirror, she saw that David continued standing there, watching her, until she turned. There was something about him that warmed her heart, but she wasn't ready for romantic feelings. The last thing she needed to do was get attached to a man, especially one who seemed to be able to read her thoughts and find a way to her heart so quickly.

As Bethany drove through town, she had to fight back the tears of nostalgia. The old-fashioned gas station with the manual pumps still stood on the corner of Elm and Broad streets, with their sign for milk, bread, and a wide assortment of candy. She'd loved going there with her grandfather to fill up the gas tank because he always rewarded her with a Milky Way or Butterfinger.

There were other things she remembered that brought back positive feelings. Bethany sometimes had a difficult time remembering the good times because there were so many earth-shattering events in her early years that knocked her for a loop. But as she passed each block and each landmark, she felt that familiar tug at her heart. This town wasn't so bad. If only her father had stuck around. If only her mother hadn't died. If only Nana hadn't had to move out the house. She sucked in a deep breath and slowly let it out as the feelings of familiarity continued to washed over her.

The day was so gorgeous and the temperature was

perfect for her to drive with the windows open. As she pulled up to the main traffic light in town, she shut her eyes for a couple of seconds and inhaled deeply once again. The aroma of freshly baked bread from the local bakery filled her nostrils. One tiny tear escaped her eyelashes.

Bethany reached up and wiped her cheek with the back of her hand. Crying wasn't something she should be doing right now. There were more pressing issues, her grandmother for one.

Nana had moved from her house to a retirement complex, where there were activities and opportunities to socialize with other people her age. Although Bethany was saddened by Nana moving from the house, she understood the reason. In fact, she was glad Nana would be with some of the old friends she hadn't had time for over the past few years.

Then, the call had come saying Nana had suffered a stroke and had to be moved to the facility's rehab center. The director was nice on the phone and he offered to let her stay in Nana's apartment although she was well below the minimum age.

"Residents are allowed to have guests and I'm sure Gertie would insist on you staying in her apartment," he'd said.

The retirement center was a big complex with several apartment buildings, a rehabilitation center, and a nursing home for residents who required more skilled care. What had attracted Nana to the place was the fact that they offered a full calendar of social events.

"I'm getting too old to handle my own schedule," Nana had told her over the phone. "All I have to do now is show up and they do it all for me."

Bethany chuckled now at Nana's choice of words.

Gertie Chalmers had never let anyone else do anything for her in the past, and she suspected that wouldn't change now. It was just a matter of time before her grandmother was the social queen of the retirement complex.

Since this was such a small town, Bethany knew most of the personnel at the retirement center, including Mr. Michaels, the director, who'd been good friends with her mother back in school. Bethany suspected Mr. Michaels had a romantic interest in her mother, but he was too much of a gentleman to say anything.

As Bethany walked through the double doors of the facility, she was greeted by one of her old high-school classmates. "Bethany, you look great!" She couldn't for the life of her remember the woman's name, but she knew the face.

Bethany smiled, in spite of how she felt. "Thanks. Have you seen my grandmother?"

"Mrs. Chalmers is in room 102, down the first hall on your left." The receptionist pointed her finger in the direction she stated, and Bethany headed that way.

Several wheelchairs were lined up outside the rooms in the hallway, and Bethany instantly recognized her grandmother. "Nana," she said, rushing toward the woman who'd always been her rock.

"Susan?" the older woman said, a puzzled look crossing her face.

Bethany stopped abruptly and pulled back, her heart twisting with pain. Susan was her mother, Nana's daughter.

"Nana," Bethany replied in a hoarse voice. "It's me, Bethany."

With a look of temporary confusion, Nana smiled

sweetly and steepled her fingers in front of her. Then, she closed her eyes and winced. "I'm so sorry, Bethany, honey. For some reason, I keep forgetting things, and I have the worst headache!"

Chapter Three

Bethany gulped. There was no way she could have been prepared for this. Yes, she knew that Nana had suffered a stroke, but she didn't expect her to appear so frail, sitting in a wheelchair with a lap robe casually tossed over her legs to keep them warm. With as much calmness as she could show, Bethany knelt down beside her grandmother and stroked her arm. "Nana, I'm sure you'll feel better soon. It takes time to heal after a stroke."

Her grandmother's smile faded, and she wrinkled her forehead as if trying to piece things together in her mind. Her heart ached. The last person she had left in her family had suffered a terrible trauma. Bethany reached out to hold her grandmother's hand.

Finally, Nana patted Bethany's hand and said, "I don't want you hanging out here all day, Bethany, honey. Why don't you run along and visit some of your old friends? I've met some new people here, and they can keep me company."

Bethany looked around at all the other faces in the hall. She recognized a few of them, but most, she didn't remember.

"Y-yes, yes, I'll do that, Nana." Bethany stood up, leaned over, kissed her grandmother's forehead, and backed away. "I'll be back tomorrow."

As soon as she was out of her grandmother's sight, she turned and ran toward the main office. Mr. Michaels was standing behind the reception desk when she rushed through the double doors. With a smile, he nodded. "Bethany, I'm glad you were able to get here so quickly. Have you seen your grandmother?"

Suddenly, all of Bethany's reserve washed away in a flood of tears. There was no way she could stop it, in spite of the fact that she didn't want anyone to see how deeply she was feeling this pain. Mr. Michaels quickly came from behind the reception desk, took her by the arm, and led her into his private office down the hall. As soon as they were inside with the door closed, he handed her a tissue.

"I know this is difficult for you, Bethany," he said as he pulled up a chair for her. "Your grandmother is getting pretty old, and things like this often happen. Our bodies fail us toward the end of our lives, and there's not a whole lot we can do about it." He stopped and studied Bethany as he sat on the edge of his desk.

"Can't you give her some medicine to make her feel better?" Bethany said, still sobbing.

He chuckled softly. "I wish it was that easy. But I can tell you one thing, her stroke wasn't all that severe. We expect her to make quite a bit of progress over the next few weeks. In fact, I wouldn't be surprised if she is up and walking around within a few weeks."

Bethany's eyebrows shot up. Hope sprang into her heart, and she smiled through the tears. "Really?"

He nodded as he glanced at his watch. "Really." Then he pulled away from his desk and headed toward the door. "Feel free to stay in here until you're ready to leave. I have the key to your grandmother's apartment at the front desk."

"Are you leaving?" she asked.

Mr. Michaels glanced at his watch again. "Yes, I'm expecting a guest in a few minutes. Why don't you stop by the multi-purpose room before you leave. I'd like for you to meet someone new to town."

Bethany's ears were ringing, but she nodded. "Thanks, Mr. Michaels."

"So you'll come?" He stood there and looked at her until she nodded.

"Sure, I'll be there. Just let me get my thoughts in order first."

Backing out, he said, "Take your time. We'll be there for a while."

Then, he left, gently closing the door behind him. Bethany thought about what Mr. Michaels had said. Her grandmother's frailty broke her heart, but there was hope. That was what the director of this place had said. Was it false hope? she wondered. After a few more sniffles, Bethany stood up and went toward the door. Her eyes were still red, but she'd agreed to meet Mr. Michaels's guest in the multi-purpose room.

She knew the general direction, so she headed there. As soon as she got to the large room in the center of the building, she stopped, her mouth falling open. Sitting in the middle of a crowd of elderly patients was David, the man who'd purchased Nana's house. And Mr. Michaels was standing at the edge of the group, smiling and laughing with them.

Bethany started to turn and run before they saw her, but she reacted too slowly. Mr. Michaels spotted her and motioned for her to join them.

Slowly, she walked over in their direction, never allowing herself to meet David's gaze. "I'm so glad you found us, Bethany," Mr. Michaels said. "I'd like for you to meet our new chaplain, David Hadaway."

"Chaplain?" Bethany asked as she looked at him questioningly. But wasn't he the pastor of New Hope?

Mr. Michaels nodded. "He so graciously volunteers his time and visits our residents whenever he can. He also does a small service on Sunday afternoons. In fact, Gertie came for the last one, since that was her first day out of bed after her stroke."

David smiled and added, "Your grandmother knew all the hymns and she sang them beautifully."

"I didn't realize she was able to go anywhere," Bethany said.

David glanced at Mr. Michaels and then back at Bethany. "In my limited experience with stroke victims, it's best to bring back as much normalcy as quickly as possible. I've seen some pretty amazing things happen in short amounts of time after the onset of this type of illness."

His gaze told her that he understood what she was going through. The warmth she felt flooding her veins made her uneasy, so she backed away. Don't get too close, she warned herself. He's already found his way into town and into your heart.

"I, uh . . ." Bethany stuttered. Then, she started over. "I didn't know you came here too."

David tilted his head. "I have a special place in my

heart for the people here." Silence fell over the room as Bethany backed away.

"Don't forget, Bethany," Mr. Michaels reminded her, "I left the key to Gertie's apartment at the front desk. Why don't you go on and get some rest. I'm sure you're probably exhausted by now." He looked at her in a fatherly way, which provided her with even more comfort. At least, they hadn't insisted on her sticking around to socialize.

David cleared his throat, capturing Bethany's attention. "You're welcome to attend church on Sunday with your grandmother. Visitors are always welcome."

Bethany didn't see how she could refuse. "Sure," she said. "I'll be here."

Mr. Michaels's eyes lit up, and he smiled. "Wonderful, Bethany. Family involvement is so important in patient recovery."

As soon as she had backed all the way to the door, Bethany turned and left as quickly as she could. Her knees were weak and her head was spinning. She was nearly outside the building when she realized she still needed the key to Nana's apartment. Mr. Michaels had said that he'd left it with the receptionist. Well, at least, she didn't have to go too far into the building to get it. She'd just have to go right back inside the door, grab the key, and she'd be gone.

What Bethany hadn't counted on was running into David as he was leaving. "Bethany," he said, that warm smile still plastered on his face. "This is really a good thing for you to be doing for your grandmother. I hope you like my church service."

"I'm sure I will," Bethany said, not daring to look him in the eye.

He stood there and waited while she got the key from

the receptionist, and when she moved toward the door, he held it for her. "Do you need any help unloading your car?"

Bethany shrugged. "I didn't bring that much stuff with me. Most of it will come on the truck in a few days. I need to rent storage space until I find a place to rent. Then, I have to take the car to the rental booth at the airport. I guess I'll use Nana's car until she recovers."

David walked along in silence with her to her car. As soon as they reached their destination, he turned to her and said, "I'm sure that's what she'd want. Why don't you keep your things at my house? I've got plenty of room."

"No," she began immediately. "I couldn't possibly do that."

"And why not?" he asked, leaning against the car door, preventing her from getting into it.

Again, she shrugged. "It wouldn't be right. Besides, I have so much stuff, you'd be swimming in clutter."

David threw his head back and laughed heartily. "That's the last thing I'd worry about. Since my nephew's been with me, clutter is my middle name."

"That's different."

His face grew somber as he reached out and took her hands in his. "Maybe it is different, but I still want you to consider my offer. It doesn't make sense to pay for storage when I've got that great big house."

"I'll think about it," Bethany said, wishing David would move away from her car so she could drive around to the back of the complex where her grandmother's apartment was. She leaned to the side and held out the keys.

He took the hint and pulled away. "If you need me, you know where to find me." He reached into his shirt pocket and pulled out a business card. "Both my home and church numbers are on here. Don't hesitate to call."

Bethany took the card, cast a quick glance at it, and smiled, allowing herself to take a long look at him. He really was nice looking. In fact, he had the sweetest expression she'd ever seen on a man. But she also suspected he wouldn't budge on his principles or moral issues. He was a man who knew right from wrong, and he had strong convictions. That attracted her even more, but she had to keep her distance. Just because David was a moral man didn't mean that he couldn't break her heart. Her emotions were so brittle right now, it wouldn't take much to do that, anyway. Nana's apartment was on the opposite end of the complex, and Bethany was thankful that it had a private entrance. One thing she valued at this time of her life was privacy. She needed to be able to pull into her cocoon when things got tough, and from the way things were going right now, it was exactly what she needed.

David shook his head as he drove back to his house—correction, his mansion. He'd never dreamed that he'd be so fortunate to be able to live in a place as wonderful and big as the house he'd bought from Gertie Chalmers. What a dear, sweet woman. Then, there was the matter of her granddaughter.

In just a few short hours, Bethany Moore had found her way into his heart, and he felt like pulling her into his arms to comfort her. He'd come close to doing that a few times, but he caught himself before he had a chance to act. David knew that he needed to get Bethany out of that area of his heart. What he needed to concentrate on now was doing his job and being a good neighbor to Bethany, especially since that was what would help Gertie more than anything else.

However, no matter how much he tried not to think about that sweet expression, the look on her face that spoke of a need for his arms around her, he couldn't. All he wanted to do ever since he'd met Bethany was to take her, hold her, and kiss her until she knew everything would be all right. The pain in her eyes pierced his heart. Not to mention the fact that her hair caught the sunlight in a shimmering glimmer, like stars in the early evening.

David took a right turn, made a circle around the block, and headed back toward the retirement center. No sense in going home when he knew he wouldn't be able to think until he had a chance to talk to Bethany again. He had to see her one more time, hopefully long enough to lose the desire to hold her. All the way there, David hummed a song he remembered from childhood, one that spoke of new found love. It was a song that hadn't particularly caught his attention in the past, but it sounded pretty good to him now. If he took a deep breath, he could almost taste the bread baking at the local bakery. It was time for dinner, but he had no desire to eat. All he wanted was to be with Bethany.

Sure, it was dangerous for him to give in to his temptation and desire to be with her right now, mainly because he was acting on impulse. This wasn't a well thought out move, but it was what he wanted to do more than anything else at the moment. But what if she didn't want to see him? She'd seemed mighty anxious to get rid of him only a few minutes ago. Well, he just wouldn't take no for an answer. He actually had a few things to discuss with her right now, so he had a perfectly good excuse if he needed one.

Gertie Chalmers had been very gracious during the

entire sales process. She'd listed the house with the most reputable realtor in town, someone who went to David's church. As soon as he received the call that the property was available, he'd jumped right into his car, driven straight there, and knocked on the door without waiting for an appointment.

At first, he'd feared that she might refuse to let him in to see the place, but as soon as he told her what he was there for and who'd sent him, she smiled, opened the door wide, and motioned for him to come right in. The second he stepped foot inside the mansion, he knew he wanted it for his own. She'd just baked gingerbread, and the aroma had filled the house, titillating his nostrils and drawing him deeper into the warmth of the old house. If David had scheduled an appointment, he would have assumed the baking was done to make the house more appealing. But he'd arrived unannounced, so this was obviously something she did on her own.

"I've just made a fresh batch of cookies. Why don't you come on into the kitchen and have one?" she'd offered.

Without hesitation, he followed her to the warm country kitchen and sat down at her table while she poured him a glass of milk and set a platter of warm gingerbread cookies before him. He'd eaten at least half a dozen before he got up and saw the rest of the house. Overlooking its state of disrepair, David envisioned all sorts of things happening in the house. He mentally placed himself repairing, decorating, and entertaining in its many rooms. It was absolutely perfect.

"But don't you need to show the house to your wife?" Gertie had asked.

With a smile, he shook his head. "I don't have one of those yet. But maybe, one of these days . . ." His voice trailed off as he reached out and felt the carved wooden banister following the stairs to the second floor that held even more wonderful surprises for him to see.

By the time he left Gertie Chalmers's house, he knew all about Bethany, the granddaughter who was revered by the kind elderly lady. He knew that Bethany was still single. It was pretty obvious that Gertie wanted him to meet her. He chuckled at the reminder of how many little old ladies wanted him to meet their young female relatives.

David snapped back to the present as he entered the gates of the retirement center's well manicured grounds. He knew that this town's elderly population was blessed to have such a nice facility. In fact, he thought this was where he'd want to be if he couldn't take care of his own house. Maybe someday. But in the meantime, he had quite a bit of living to do.

Within a few minutes, David pulled into the driveway of Gertie's apartment. It was in a building at the end of the street with a doorway overlooking a preserve that provided privacy for her. He was glad that she didn't have to go directly from the house to the nursing home. It would have been much more traumatic for her. David got out of his car and walked up the sidewalk, mentally rehearsing what he needed to say when Bethany answered the door. But he wasn't prepared for what stood before him.

Her eyes widened as she recognized him. "David?"

He gulped. Bethany had changed into black leggings and a long lime green sweater that was in direct contrast with her strawberry blond hair. She was even more striking in casual clothes than she'd been wearing a dress. He was rendered temporarily speechless.

She blinked her eyes. "Did you forget something?"

"Uh, yeah," he said, forcing himself to run through a list of things he could have forgotten. "I wanted to see if you were available to come to dinner tonight. Jonathan and I would love to have someone different to talk to."

His heart turned upside down as she hesitated, licking her lips and making him feel weak at the knees. For the first time since he'd become an adult, David had the sensation of being infatuated with a female. It made him smile. He'd been attracted to women many times, but this feeling almost reminded him of being sixteen all over again. Bethany looked a little bit nervous at first, so he took a step back.

"Are you sure you don't mind?" she asked. She still looked nervous, and now that it appeared that she might accept his invitation, he was too.

"Of course, I don't mind. In fact, I insist." He stepped away from the door and closed it behind him. "Why don't you come with me now, and Jonathan and I can take you back home."

Bethany stood there and studied him, her eyes widening and then becoming narrow as she inhaled deeply. David couldn't remember ever seeing anyone going through so much inner turmoil in such a short amount of time. He was glad he'd come back.

"Okay, let me get my purse," she said as she took a step back.

Then, as if in slow motion, her heel stuck on the edge of the rug, she lost her balance, and he instinctively reached out to grab her. He instantly felt the sparks, and he knew that he'd have some serious soul searching to do after dinner. But that could be dealt with later. He still had a couple of hours to spend with this wonderful creature, and he couldn't have been more thrilled.

"Hold onto my arm, Bethany," David said as soon as

she was ready to go. "I don't want to have to leave your grandmother's nursing home bed, only to have to turn around and visit you in the hospital."

She chuckled, her laughter deep and husky. David felt another one of those electric pangs shoot through him, and he tightened his grip on her.

"Nana will be pleased that you stopped by and invited me to have dinner with you." Her voice was on the edge of a breath, which unnerved him to the point of making him realize he was in trouble. At least he knew he was still a red-blooded American man. He was beginning to wonder if the stress of the ministry was getting to him and taking away his desire for the feel of a woman by his side. Now he knew it was still there.

As they got to his car, he stopped, turned her toward him, and gazed at her for a long moment. "Bethany, I'm not only doing this to please your grandmother."

She looked back into his eyes and blinked before she allowed her gaze to settle back on his. "I know you're not."

"You do?" David's heart skipped a beat. Bethany could have reached out and knocked him over with a feather.

Nodding, she sighed. "You're doing it because you want me to go to your church."

Chapter Four

David stopped in his tracks and stared at Bethany, his chin hanging to his chest, his mouth wide open. "Is that what you think?"

With a serene smile, Bethany nodded. "Hey, David, don't worry about it. I understand."

For the first time he could remember in a long time, David felt a deep-seated anger. "If you think I'm using underhanded tactics to get you to join my church, then you're all wrong, Bethany." He had to bite his tongue to keep from saying anything stronger than that.

Still grinning, she took his arm and led him to his car. "I told you, I understand. I've been thinking about it, and I know that this is what you're supposed to do."

"What I'm supposed to do?" David's voice squeaked. He'd never been so insulted in his life. He was *not* the manipulative type.

"Sure," she said when they reached his car. "Be nice to the new people in town so they'll join the church. How else do you expect the collection plates to be full, especially since the congregation is probably getting way up there in age, from what I remember."

David had to take a deep breath and exhale slowly in order to see straight. In just a few short moments he'd gone from fantasizing about him and Bethany falling in love to feeling a rage he hadn't experienced since his hormones settled down in his early twenties.

"Before we go any further, Bethany, let me set a few things straight."

Her eyes widened and then she blinked, holding them wide again. "Yes?"

"First of all, I don't do things like that. If I want you to come to church, I come right out and ask you. When I invite you over for dinner, that's all that's on my agenda. Nothing else." He stopped talking and stared at her, hoping she'd get the point in full.

"Nothing else?" she asked, her face held in animated suspense. "But of course, you wouldn't turn me down if I asked you questions about your church, would you?"

"Well . . ." He blew out another exasperated breath. "Of course, not."

"There ya go." She turned and faced his car while he stood there helplessly fumbling for the right key.

They rode in silence for a few minutes before he stopped at a red light and turned to face her. "You think you have this whole thing figured out, don't you?"

David had noticed a complete change in her demeanor, which meant one of two things. Either she'd come to some sort of conclusion about him, or she was putting on an act. Both choices, as far as he was concerned, were bad ones. Neither of them was open and honest, another reason he shouldn't fall in love with her.

"Yes, I think so, David." She straightened her seatbelt as she shifted in her seat to face him.

David knew he had his work cut out for him. He would have thought that he would have lost interest in her after the comments she'd made, but he hadn't. She could let her guard down and be herself, allowing things to be shown at face value—not everyone had to play games to get through life.

They rode in silence to his house. David didn't want to risk saying something that could be misconstrued, so he figured being quiet was probably best. Once in a while, he sneaked a glance over at Bethany, and she just sat there, staring straight ahead. Each time he looked at her, he saw a different expression, going from a contemplative gaze to the pained look of an agonizing memory. Too bad he couldn't just say something comforting that would make her feel better instantly. But that would be too easy, he thought.

He finally pulled into the driveway and turned to Bethany. "I know you don't completely trust me, but please try to have a good time."

"Of course, I will, David," she said. "Just because you've got ulterior motives doesn't mean you're a bad guy. In fact, you're actually pretty nice."

He let out a chuckle, in spite of the twist he felt in his chest. "I guess I'll have to settle for being pretty nice. But that wasn't what I had in mind." Oh, man, he hadn't meant for that to slip out.

Bethany quickly turned and faced him, her eyes holding the startled look of a deer in headlights. "What, exactly, did you have in mind?"

An excited child came bouncing across the yard from the neighbor's house. "Uncle Dave! Look! I caught a frog!" Saved by the kid!

The little boy held his hand out and showed David his

prize. Bethany came forward, not appearing the least big squeamish. "That's a tree frog."

"Aren't you afraid of them?" David asked.

"No," she said, her mouth twisted in humor. "Why should I be?"

"I thought most females hated frogs and other slimy things."

Bethany's laughter sounded like windchimes on a breezy day. David's heart thudded against his chest with emotion he hadn't felt in a long, long time. She bent over and took the frog from Jonathan.

"Have you named him yet?" she asked, much to his astonishment.

Jonathan looked up at her and grinned; the gaping hole where he'd lost a tooth showed through his incredibly large smile. David hadn't seen the child grin like that since he'd arrived. "No, not yet. I'm not sure what to name a frog."

"How about Prince?"

"Prince?" Jonathan asked. "Why Prince?"

Bethany handed Jonathan back his frog and brushed her hands together as she took a step back to look at David. "Haven't you ever read fairy tales?"

"Fairy tales?" David asked. What was she getting at?

"Yeah. In fairy tales, when the girl kisses the frog, he turns into a prince."

Nodding and chuckling, David understood. "Oh, I get it."

Jonathan was still grinning. "Okay, we'll call him Prince. But I have a bunch more in a jar out back. Let's name them, so they don't feel left out."

He reached out and took Bethany's hand to take her around to the back of the house, leaving David standing there feeling silly. He'd planned to have Bethany over for dinner, hoping his nephew would go to bed early so he could get to know her better. And now, the little boy was snaking his date with the lure of a frog, of all things.

At least, Bethany was out of her blue funk. She'd seemed so sad earlier, and he wondered how to pull her out of it. Something had happened to her before he'd arrived to pick her up, and like magic, she was perky. But he didn't believe in magic. What had come over her? Bethany followed Jonathan Hadaway to the backyard. He saw her avoid looking at the tiny tree that had been planted to replace her old giant oak. After her earlier mood, the last thing she needed was to backslide into her melancholia.

"Look, lady, here's my collection of frogs." Bethany glanced over to the wooden table where there were several jars of bugs and amphibians, all packed in mayonnaise jars with holes punched in the lids.

David appeared at the edge of the porch. "Jonathan, this is Miss Moore. Not lady."

The little boy looked up at Bethany. "Sorry, Miss Moore."

With a glance toward David for approval, Bethany said, "If it's all right with your uncle, you may call me Bethany."

David shrugged. "That's fine with me, if you don't mind."

Bethany sat down and admired the collection of frogs. She patiently listened as he excitedly explained where he'd captured each and every one of them. She stood up and inspected the contents of the jar before frowning. "I think they might be sad about something, Jonathan."

"Sad?" he said as he took the jar from her hands.

Bethany nodded. "Looks like some of these frogs are

just babies, right out of the tadpole stage. They miss their families."

Still looking at the frogs, Jonathan slowly began to unscrew the lid. "I don't want them to be sad," he said. "Should I let them go?" His look of complete and total trust in Bethany touched David's heart like nothing else possibly could.

She smiled and hesitated before slowly nodding. "I know you'd take very good care of them, Jonathan, but their moms probably wonder what happened to them. It might be time for their dinner, and they don't want to miss that."

"No," Jonathan agreed, shaking his head and removing the lid. He turned the jar upside down and let the frogs hop free. "I want them to grow up to be big, strong frogs."

As David continued to watch, he knew that Bethany had woven a web of trust around his nephew. Obviously, this wasn't a problem for Bethany.

During dinner, Jonathan glanced up at Bethany with open admiration, letting her know that she was welcome at their table. Bethany seemed to thoroughly enjoy his attention, so David didn't even try to capture any of it. He just sat there and enjoyed watching Bethany and Jonathan interact.

Finally, after dessert, David stood up and motioned to Jonathan. "Grab your plates, sport, and take them to the sink. You need to get your bath and go to bed. We have a big day tomorrow."

Jonathan grinned at Bethany and said, "Uncle Dave's taking a bunch of kids on a hike tomorrow. Wanna go?"

David cleared his throat. "Uh, Jonathan, why don't you give Bethany a break? I'm sure she's tired from all that traveling. Maybe some other time." He didn't dare look at Bethany who just stood there and watched him.

After Jonathan did as he was told and headed for the stairs, Bethany said, "If you need to go help him, I can clean the kitchen."

"You're the guest. I don't expect you to do any of the work." David continued to clear the table in a way that showed Bethany he'd done this many times before. "Jonathan has had to do so much on his own, I don't think he'd know what to do if I went up there to help him."

"How long has he been with you?" Bethany asked.

"A couple of weeks. But before that, he was with his mother, who had to work after my brother left them. Little Jonathan came home every day after school to an empty house, and he always started dinner."

Bethany gasped. David saw her shock as she glanced toward the kitchen door as if she expected the little boy to appear suddenly. "He's so young."

David nodded. "I know. That's why I agreed to take him until they got their problems worked out."

"But what about school?"

"I've got a couple of the moms from church tutoring him, using the curriculum from his teacher back home. If we have to, we'll switch him to the schools in town, but I don't want to bring any more changes in his young life if I don't have to."

Bethany shook her head. "Here, let me wash that pan."

He pulled it away from her and lowered it into soapy water.

"Oh, but I want to," she said as she nudged him out of the way.

Together, they managed to clean the kitchen very quickly, mostly in silence. David knew that Bethany was thinking about the plight of the little boy in his care.

While David felt sorry for Jonathan, he knew that it could have been much worse. At least the kid had an uncle who loved him. That was more than Bethany obviously felt right now.

Bethany's heart went out to little Jonathan. Here was a young boy who was hurting, and she knew exactly how he felt. She'd experienced a similar pain after her parents' divorce, with one major difference. Her mother hadn't sent her off to live with a relative. She'd come along as well. The irony of the situation wasn't lost on Bethany. This was the same house where she'd found refuge from her own inner turmoil. She and Jonathan had quite a bit in common. Too bad he didn't have a big oak tree to climb.

"David," Bethany said as she wrung out the dishrag.

"Yes?" He turned to her and caused her heart to skip a beat. Better watch it, she warned herself. He's a preacher who only wants to look good for his church. There's no reason to get excited over all this attention.

"I used to have a treehouse when I was Jonathan's age."

David smiled. "Yes, I know. Your grandmother showed me pictures."

The visual image of the treehouse made Bethany smile. "I know that you can't build a treehouse in that little tree yet, but maybe we can come up with something close."

"Like what?" David said. He took a few steps closer to her, and she felt the breath catch in her throat. What was happening to her?

Bethany shrugged, forcing the lump from her throat. It settled in her chest, and she coughed. "I don't know. Maybe a playhouse or something else he can hide in."

"You know, that sounds like a pretty good idea. Maybe I can build him one. I still have some wood left over."

"Be sure to let him help you so he'll feel like it's his," Bethany said.

As he took her hands in his, she felt her insides turn to mush. "You're such a wise person, Bethany. I feel very fortunate that you came into my life."

"Really?" she asked, forgetting to be suspicious of his motives. Sure, she was still aware of who he was and why she was here, but she wanted to think he wasn't lying to her.

"Yes, absolutely. I've been trying to figure out how to draw my nephew out of his shell without much success, and you came along and did it the first day you met him."

Bethany felt her face heat with embarrassment. "It's nothing. I was a kid once."

"Me, too, but you didn't see me naming his frogs, did you?"

With a light chuckle, Bethany shook her head. "I just figured you probably never had frogs for pets."

"I've been trying to get him to set those frogs free, and he wouldn't listen to me. You didn't even have to beg," David continued.

She remembered her grandfather saying her exact words to her when she had a jar full of frogs. "I have more experience, that's all." She wasn't about to give away her secrets just yet. At least, not until she had a chance to feel this emotion a few more times.

"Then, let me thank you again," he said, jostling her from her short tour down memory lane.

"Think nothing of it."

Bethany backed away from David, pulling her hands free. She needed to catch her breath, and the only way she could do that was to keep from touching him. Her hands still felt warm where they were enveloped in his, and she clasped them together so she could think. She walked around the room and looked at all the trophies and decorations on the shelves her grandfather had built. "Are all these yours?"

He nodded as he crossed the room and joined her. "Most of them, yes. A few of them belong to my brother, but he doesn't have a permanent residence right now. At least, not until he and his wife straighten things out."

Bethany picked up one statue of a baseball glove holding a ball. "You played baseball?"

"First base," he answered. "My college team went to the state finals."

She grinned at him. "That's great. I played intramural softball, but we weren't that good."

"What position?" he asked with a look that indicated he was more interested in something other than her softball skills.

"Usually shortstop. Sometimes catcher." Bethany stood there and let his deepening gaze pull her in. Her heart nearly stopped as they stood there and stared at each other.

Not moving a single facial muscle other than his mouth, David answered, "Those are important positions. They can make or break the game."

Bethany gulped. She had a feeling that he wasn't only talking about softball now. There was something in the way he looked at her that made her mouth feel dry. He quickly closed the gap between them, and she felt a warmth flood her veins as he took the statue, glanced at it for a second, and returned it to the shelf. Then, he took her hands in his and pulled her to his chest.

"Bethany, I hope you don't take this the wrong way, but I want to get to know you better."

She had a feeling that there was something between them, but until he actually said it, she could pretend it was nothing. At first, she just stood there, stunned. But as she forced her mind to think rationally, she pulled her hands free.

Chapter Five

"Bethany?" David stopped his progression toward her and studied her for a moment.

She spun around to face him. "David, I really need to get back to my grandmother's apartment right now. I'm confused."

"I didn't mean—" he began. Then, when he looked really closely at her face, the anguish he'd somehow missed before, he knew that no matter what he said, nothing would change for them tonight. He sighed and nodded, reaching into his pocket for the car keys. "Okay. Let me grab the next door neighbor to watch Jonathan. I'll be right back."

Rather than call, David went to his neighbor's house and knocked on the door. While he waited, he ran the events of the day through his mind and tried to figure out where he went wrong. The more he thought about it, the more he realized he hadn't done anything he should have to make Bethany trust him. He knew, from his experience as a pastor, that some people were slow to warm up to someone in his position and he just needed to chill out. Let them see him in action and quit trying to impress them with his honesty and integrity.

As soon as he got the woman next door to sit in the house until he came home, David motioned for Bethany to go ahead outside to the car. "I shouldn't be too long. If he wakes up, just tell him I'll be right back."

His neighbor smiled and winked at Bethany. "Take your time, David. My husband's home with my brood, and I'll enjoy having the peace and quiet. I still want to know your secret as to how you get Jonathan to bed so early."

"I don't give him a choice," David said as he closed the door.

Bethany was already in the car when he went outside. He saw her silhouette against the moonlit sky, and he couldn't help but notice how wonderful her profile was—strong jaw, adorable upturned nose, eyes that always seemed to be open wide with astonishment.

"I should have brought my car," Bethany said, making an obvious effort to not look at him. "That way, you wouldn't have had to go to so much trouble."

David had already turned the key in the ignition and put the car in reverse. He hesitated for a moment, then put it back into park. "Bethany, let's get one thing straight. What I do for you is no trouble at all. I do it because I want to do it—not to add members to the church, not to make your grandmother happy, not to impress anyone with my willingness to do anything."

She'd turned and looked him in the eye as he spoke. There was a small amount of moisture glistening in her eyes, making him wonder if she was about to start crying. Why did he keep saying things to upset her?

David kept his mouth shut most of the way, not wanting to make her feel bad anymore. She certainly deserved good treatment, after coming all this way to be with her grandmother. He'd always appreciated when people had a strong sense of family.

One thing he knew for certain was that her grandmother loved Bethany. Gertie had beamed with pride as she showed him pictures of her, her husband, Bethany's mother, and Bethany from years ago after they'd come away from the sanctuary. "My daughter and granddaughter looked so pretty, my husband had one of his friends snap this so I could look at it later," Gertie had said with tears in her eyes. "Now that Susan's gone, I'm glad he did that. I miss my only child." David had a tremendous amount of sympathy for Gertie.

As he pulled into the retirement center complex, he slowed way down. The posted speed was much lower than on the regular road surrounding the gated community. He easily found his way to the apartment, pulled up in front of the unit, and stopped. "Bethany," he said as softly as he could. "Thank you for coming tonight."

She looked at him for a split second and then cast her glance away. "I enjoyed dinner. I'm the one who should be thanking you."

Not wanting to frighten her, he reached out and gently touched her arm. "I appreciate how you handled Jonathan."

"You're welcome," she said softly.

David noticed that Bethany didn't make a move to get out of his car, so he figured she must not be ready to be alone. "Friends?" he asked, as he gazed at her, longing for an answer.

Slowly, she nodded, and her body relaxed. He let out a sigh of relief.

"Bethany, try hard not to worry too much about your grandmother."

He watched her as she allowed herself a brief glimpse of his face before she cast her eyes downward. "That's easy for you to say."

David knew that it was time for her to go inside. He got out, went around to her side of the car, and held the door while she stepped out.

"You don't have to do this, you know," she said as they walked up the sidewalk to her grandmother's apartment.

"But I want to." He stopped, took her elbow, and turned her to face him. "It's the right thing to do, Bethany." David licked his lips, and he wondered if she got what he was trying to say. He wanted to tell her that he felt something for her and that it wasn't something to take lightly. But the timing wasn't right.

Bethany tilted her head forward, raised her eyebrows, and forced a smile. "Yes, sometimes the right thing is the hardest, though."

David had no idea what she meant by that, but he could only guess. He held the screen door while she found the key. Then, once she was inside, he turned and headed back to his car. As soon as a light came on inside, he started the car and headed back home. It was time to do a little personal assessment of his feelings for her. This whole situation had blindsided him, and he needed to think about it. The last thing he'd expected to happen was to have romantic feelings for Gertie Chalmers's granddaughter.

Bethany stood in front of the window in the still dark bedroom, watching as David pulled away. He drove very slowly through the complex, respecting the posted speeds. As much as she hated to admit it, she'd found this man immensely attractive, and she wanted to get closer to him. But she couldn't allow that to happen. It was too much, too soon.

Bethany sank down on the edge of the bed as she thought about David, the house, and the little boy he was taking care of. Obviously, David loved his family.

As much as Bethany knew it was dangerous to go back to Nana's old house, she knew that she had to go back for Jonathan's sake. He needed an understanding person who could help him through what he had to deal with. Divorce was never easy on children. Besides, Bethany knew that she couldn't spend every waking moment with her grandmother.

Bethany had her bags piled up in the tiny dining room. She wondered where in the world she'd keep all her other things once they arrived. There definitely wasn't enough space in this tiny apartment, and from what she remembered, big business hadn't found its way into town enough to warrant rows and rows of storage rental units like she'd seen in the big city. Surely, though, there must be someplace she could keep her things until she found her own job and apartment once she decided to move on.

David had offered her grandmother's house. Correction, his house. He was right. There was plenty of room, and she'd know where her things were and that they wouldn't be sitting around gathering mildew in some damp, dark storage unit. But if she did that, wouldn't she owe David something? Maybe he figured that she'd come to church out of gratitude.

Bethany walked back over to the window and looked outside. She saw a crescent moon and millions of stars, all looking down at her, watching over the earth while it lay still in darkness. It was late. She needed to rest.

Never in a million years had Bethany figured on things getting this complicated. At least, she didn't think she'd have to deal with feelings for a man when she should be spending her time worrying over Nana. That was what she was here for, wasn't it? Bethany was worried that she wouldn't find sleep, but it didn't take long once her head hit the pillow. She was tired. No, she was exhausted, strung out, and without an ounce of energy. She'd been through entirely too much for one day.

Her night was filled with dreams, but not one of them made sense. Each time she awoke from a different one, she had to look around to remind herself of where she was, then force herself to go back to sleep. By the time Bethany got up the next morning, she felt like she'd spent the night in a ring with Hulk Hogan—on the opposing team. Every muscle in her body ached, and her head hurt. Her mind felt fuzzy. She knew she'd have a hard time concentrating on what she needed to do now.

Nana was always good about keeping her pantry filled with plenty of nutritious foods as well as plenty of goodies. She also had coffee and creamers in every assortment of flavors you could imagine. Hopefully, that hadn't changed since she'd moved here.

Bethany got out of bed and padded to the tiny kitchen. She opened all the cupboard doors and found what she needed to make a pot of coffee. She soon located everything she was looking for, and within a very few minutes, she was sitting down in front of a bowl of cereal, a cup of coffee, and the newspaper that had been delivered to the front door. Nana hadn't given up any of her favorite things, Bethany was happy to note. She just had them on a smaller scale.

The front page news was the same old depressing stuff, so Bethany flipped through to get to the local news. She wanted to see if she recognized any newsworthy names. As her eyes scanned the pages, she noticed a few politicians' names that had been in the news ever since she could remember. They were still up to the same old things.

She saw the huge retail ads that took over at least a third of the paper. Some of the same stores were in business, as well as a few new ones.

She kept turning the pages, scanning each column, until she reached the section titled "Religion." Without thinking, she looked down the long list of churches until she found New Hope. Her heart did a kerplunk as she spotted David Hadaway's name in bold letters, right above the times of worship service.

Bethany's ears rang as she sat there and stared at David's name. He had made such an impact on her that she couldn't take her eyes off his church's ad. At the bottom of the enclosed box was the statement, "Come as you are. Casual, friendly, welcoming atmosphere where you can worship in comfort."

Why did seeing his name make her heart do all these crazy things? She'd only met the man yesterday, for heaven's sake. Sure, he was nice. He'd done his best to make her feel welcome in his house that used to be hers, but he was one of those people who was nice to everyone. He had to be, didn't he? He was a preacher.

She got up and poured herself another cup of coffee. When she got back to the table, she saw that the paper around the ad had been wrinkled, as if she'd wadded it up in her hands. As carefully as she could, Bethany tore the paper around the ad, then set it to the side. She figured she'd need to visit his church, after all the hospi-

tality he'd extended when she'd arrived unannounced.
That was the least she could do. One time. And maybe,
once she got settled and had a chance to spend a little
time with Nana, she might think about either making
dinner for him and Jonathan, or taking them out.

Right now, though, Bethany needed to get up and start
getting ready for the day. The nursing home had several
visiting periods, and one of them was early morning,
right after breakfast. Then, most of the people either had
to take their physical therapy or get some rest before
lunch. She figured she'd better hurry up so she wouldn't
miss a chance to see Nana.

As Bethany dressed for the day, she let her mind wan-
der. The old house still looked stately at the end of the
cul-de-sac, and she had to admit, that fresh coat of paint
on the porch railing made it sparkle. He'd done a nice
job with the stairs, and although she had fond memories
of the squeaky stairs, he was right, they needed to be
repaired. Other than that, everything was still pretty
much the same. With the exception of the tree, of course.
Her stomach tightened. That tree had meant a lot to Bethany. It was something she'd always remembered being
there, and it had given her a sense of peace. A sense of
shelter. A sense of permanence, something that she
didn't feel much of as a child.

Bethany had always wondered what it would have
been like to have a doting father, one who picked her up
from school on special days so they could spend the rest
of the afternoon together. Her childhood friend, Denise,
had a father who did that once in a while, and Bethany
always noticed the sparkle in her friend's eyes when she
had that to look forward to.

Denise even offered to share her daddy with Bethany.
Thinking back on that childlike conversation, Bethany

had to smile. It was so touching, but at the time, she'd acted like she didn't need a father. In fact, she'd just laughed and said, "Who needs a daddy?" Of course, Bethany didn't believe her own words, but she was thankful for the loving family she had.

Finally, Bethany was dressed and ready to go. She headed out the door and toward her rental car when she remembered that she needed to return it to the rental booth. Somehow, she'd have to figure out how to do this. Someone needed to give her a ride back to Nana's apartment. Since Nana obviously wasn't going anywhere, Bethany could use her car until she had a chance to figure out what to do next.

The lobby of the nursing home was filled with visitors, making it difficult for Bethany to see where she was going. She had to wait behind a large group to get to the receptionist so she could let them know she was there.

Finally, she found her grandmother, who'd just finished her breakfast in her room. "Nana, why didn't you go to the dining room this morning?" she asked as she crossed the room, walking around the bed by the door that lay empty.

Nana looked at her with confusion. Then, a smile spread across her face. "Hi, Bethany. It's so good to see you! I was afraid I'd dreamed that you came by yesterday." She held out her arms, and Bethany found herself enfolded in the familiar warmth of the arms of her grandmother who'd brought her so much comfort all her life. Tears sprang to her eyes.

Chapter Six

Bethany tried to hide her tears, but Nana pulled away and took a long look at her. The woman's face tightened, and she looked like she was trying hard to maintain her composure.

Tears stung the backs of Bethany's eyes as she stood there in front of the woman she'd known all her life. Nana's physical frailties stabbed at her heart. The pain in her chest was unbearable. How could this have happened?

"Bethany." She jumped at the sound of the familiar man's voice behind her. It was David. She knew before she even turned around. What was he doing here?

Bethany stood still as she listened to his footsteps getting closer. He touched her shoulder and she flinched. Her body was tense and ultra-sensitive.

"Good morning, Gertie," David said as he walked right past Bethany and headed straight for her grandmother. "How are you feeling this morning?"

Nana looked up at David with open admiration and

batted her eyes. "Are we having church this morning, David?"

David glanced back and forth between Nana and Bethany, looking slightly confused. Bethany could tell he was uncomfortable and wondered if he'd interrupted something important.

He quickly recovered and turned back to Nana. "Gertie, your granddaughter came all this way to spend time with you." He motioned for Bethany to take a few steps closer. "She looks so much like you, I'm having a hard time figuring out which one is the grandmother and which is the granddaughter."

Gertie waved her hand at the wrist and chuckled. "Oh, you." Then, she smiled at Bethany again and reached for her. "Let me get another look at my granddaughter."

Bethany took another step closer, fully aware that David was watching every single move. When she got to her grandmother's wheelchair, she stopped and looked down.

Nana extended her arms, and Bethany leaned over for a hug. As they pulled apart, Nana looked directly into her eyes and said, "You look so much like your mother, I can hardly believe it's you, Bethany."

Not only were there tears in Nana's eyes, Bethany had to choke hers back to keep from falling apart right in front of David. She'd always known that she resembled her mother, who in turn, looked just like hers.

David squeezed Nana's shoulder and said, "I'd like to borrow your granddaughter for a moment, Gertie, if you don't mind. I'll bring her right back."

"Sure, David," she replied coyly. "Go right ahead. I need to straighten up around here, anyway."

Bethany took a quick glimpse around Nana's room and wondered what she was talking about. The place was spic and span. It was obvious the housekeeping staff was doing an excellent job. She allowed David to pull her out of the room, down the hall, and into a large room that was obviously meant for recreational activities but was currently unoccupied. He stopped when he was out of hearing distance from anyone else.

"I know how this must hurt, Bethany," he said softly.

Bethany glared at David. "No, you don't."

He shut his eyes. Bethany wished she could be anywhere but where she was right now. The last thing she needed was some do-gooder, who didn't have a clue as to what deep, emotional pain really felt like, to tell her how she was feeling.

"Okay, Bethany, so I don't know. But I think I can help you."

"How?" She cocked her head to one side and openly stared at him.

David took a deep breath, letting it out as he spoke. Bethany saw that he was walking on eggshells. He didn't want to say the wrong thing. "I've had years of experience in dealing with people who have suffered from physical injuries and illnesses that cause loss of normal activity."

Bethany let out a snort. "So, you're a jack of all trades, huh? I thought you were just a preacher."

"My first job out of seminary was in a veteran's hospital, where I saw almost everything you could possibly see. Most of the problems there were from injuries suffered at war, so there was generally bitterness attached."

"My grandmother was never in a war," Bethany said. "She's always been the rock in my life, and now she can't do much of anything."

He shifted his weight from one foot to another, and then he reached out and tilted Bethany's chin so she could face him. "Bethany, I think it's wonderful that she's always been there for you, but she's still a human being, complete with frailties and a human body that won't last forever."

"It's not supposed to be that way," Bethany said, now letting the tears fall. She couldn't hold them back any longer.

"It seems wrong, but we all have storms in our lives."

"I've had plenty of those in my life."

"We all have, Bethany. Granted, some more than others, but no one's life is immune to the trials and tribulations in the world."

"That's all I've had," Bethany said.

"I beg to differ," he said.

"Oh, yeah, once in a while something good happens, but then along comes the evil monster to take it all away."

David took both of her hands in his and squeezed them. She looked at him as he spoke again. "You've been loved by your wonderful grandmother, a grandfather, and a mother. Sure, you've had a lot of tragedy, but that's part of life."

Shaking her head, Bethany said, "I don't know. It just seems as though some people lead charmed lives, and they don't ever have to deal with bad times."

"I haven't met anyone like that yet," David said.

"My friend, Denise, is one who has never had anything awful occur in her life. It seems like everything she touches turns to gold. Her parents stayed married, and she stayed here in town because she was so happy."

"Denise?" he asked, taking one hand away from hers and rubbing his chin. "You wouldn't happen to be talking about Denise Carson, would you?"

Her head jerked up as she realized he knew exactly who she was talking about. "Yes. Do you know her?"

With a grin, he nodded. "Denise was one of the first people I met when I came to town."

Bethany should have known that. Denise was the type of person who never met a stranger. In fact, whenever a new girl arrived at school, she was the first one to invite her over to play. "Denise was my best friend growing up, but she never really understood what I went through." Bethany couldn't remember anything bad ever happening to her friend. "We had some really nice times."

"See?" he said. "I knew that not everything in your life was bad, Bethany. Denise Carson was special to you, and you have wonderful memories of your times together."

Nodding, Bethany forced a grin. "Yeah, I guess you're right. I need to call her."

David put both hands on his hips and took a step back. "Tell you what, if you can wait about an hour while I visit a few of my church members here, I'll take you to her store."

"You've been there?" Bethany asked.

"Of course," he replied. "I helped her get started."

So, he liked books, she thought. That was another thing she and David had in common.

Bethany and David walked back to the hall together, where they parted and went in two different directions. "I'll meet you by the reception desk in an hour, Bethany. Please go easy on yourself with your grandmother. She's been through a very rough thing with that stroke, but recovery looks good."

Nodding, Bethany backed toward Nana's room.

Nana's eyes lit up as she entered the room. "Bethany,

how do you like David? I figured the two of you would hit it off."

"He's nice, Nana," Bethany replied. She had to change the subject. "But I'm here to help you get better."

Nana flipped her hand at the wrist. "I've never felt better in my life."

Bethany forced a smile. "That's good, Nana." She fidgeted as she glanced around the room, trying hard to think of something to keep her grandmother from going back to the subject of David.

A nurse appeared in the doorway right then, and Bethany let out a sigh of relief. "Time for your medication, Mrs. Chalmers."

Bethany stepped back and let the nurse come forward to do her job. She stood there, watching as the woman who'd been her solid rock most of her life sat there as an invalid. Nothing could have hurt more.

On her way out, the nurse turned to Bethany and said, "Why don't you visit with her for just a few more minutes, then give her a chance to rest before you come back?"

Bethany nodded. That was the nurse's nice way of telling her that it was almost time to leave. At least, David would be waiting for her. She actually looked forward to seeing her old friend, Denise, and since she wasn't sure where the bookstore was, it was nice for David to show her.

He was waiting in the reception area, just like he'd told her he would be. "How's she doing?"

Bethany shrugged. "About the same, I guess."

"She's doing better every day."

Bethany tilted her head and took a long look at David. He seemed so calm about this, but why shouldn't he be? It wasn't his grandmother lying in the nursing home bed.

All the way to Denise's store, David chatted about the new businesses in town. He'd only been here a short time, but he seemed to have a good feel for the pulse of Clearview.

Once they got to Main Street, he slowed way down and began looking for a parking space. Bethany noticed the new parking meters that had been designed to look like antiques. The streetlights matched, and the banners that hung from them depicted the season. It was absolutely charming, what had been done since she'd been away, which now seemed like a very long time.

"Here we go," David said as he swung into a space. "Let me feed the meter, and we can go see Denise."

Bethany waited while David fished in his pocket for correct change. He joined her on the red brick sidewalk, and together, they headed north toward the town square. There was a new, understated, elegant charm in Clearview. Some of the old businesses were still there, such as Tony's Drug Store. The barber shop had been replaced by a piece goods shop, specializing in country patterns and fabrics. Antique stores graced nearly every corner, and in between were various service-oriented businesses, such as accounting offices and lawyers. It was much more upscale than it was in the past when half the stores were either deserted or on the verge of bankruptcy.

"Here we are," David said, stopping in front of a tiny but elegant bookstore.

"This is Denise's store?" Bethany asked, suddenly feeling her pulse in her throat.

"What's the matter?" David asked. "Afraid?"

Bethany nodded.

Denise had always been the cheerful, happy-go-lucky person who'd managed to pull her out of her frequent bad moods. She always had that devil-may-care attitude that made it all but impossible for Bethany to envision her friend being this responsible. But just as David had said, Denise stood behind the counter, her familiarity heartwarming but frightening at the same time.

She glanced up when she heard the bells jingling on the door. It took a couple of seconds for her to realize who'd just walked in, but when she did, she let out a loud squeal. "Bethany!"

Next thing she knew, her friend's arms were around her neck—a friend she'd neglected to keep in contact with over the years. And obviously, a friend who still cared about her.

"Bethany," she repeated as she held her at arm's length. "Let me get a good look at you." With a huge smile on her face, she gave Bethany the once-over and then hugged her again. "You haven't changed a bit."

Bethany gulped. "You haven't either." Well, with the exception of one thing.

"Actually, I've changed quite a bit. I'd love to tell you all about it, but I can't right now with the store open." She gestured around the store. "What do you think?"

Bethany glanced around the room and noticed that everything seemed very organized and well thought out. "It's very nice. I didn't know you went for this kind of thing."

With a chuckle and a quick exchanged glance with David, Denise said, "I didn't either, until I met David. It was amazing what happened."

Bethany suddenly felt a rush of adrenaline. Was there a relationship between Denise and David? A feeling dangerously close to jealousy hovered over her, but she forced herself to smile.

"You settled down and actually started reading?"

Bethany said after getting a grip on herself. "It's very amazing."

David stood there and watched the two of them, a fact that Bethany was painfully aware of. She figured that he must have had some sort of emotional attachment to Denise to be able to tolerate their reunion. Most men would have left by now, after all the squeals that came from her friend.

"Let me take you on a quick tour of the store," Denise said, taking Bethany by the hand. "The front of the store is mostly for bestsellers, gift items, and promotional things. Back here, we have fiction, and in that corner is the children's section. The very back of the store has a sound room for music and videos." It was all so organized.

"Looks like you're doing very well," Bethany said as she took it all in. "How long have you been here?"

"A little over a year," she said breathlessly. "And get this. We're close to turning a profit, and we're only in our second year."

"That's phenomenal," Bethany agreed. "You must have a good business mind."

"I try."

Bethany had seen the whole store, and she still couldn't believe what had happened to her friend. The transformation was incredible, given the fact that both she and Denise had gone through a rather wild phase their last couple of years in high school. In fact, Nana had even forbidden her to be with Denise on a few occasions, when she knew that the two of them were up to no good.

Nana and her mother had breathed a sigh of relief when Bethany and Denise had been accepted by two different colleges. And after a year, Bethany heard that Denise had flunked out of school and had returned to Clearview to work as a teller at one of the banks. Bethany, on the other hand, had remained in school and excelled in accounting, which was what she got her degree in.

"Promise you'll call me once you get settled," Denise said as they walked back to the front of the store. "I have someone else come in to run the store on Wednesdays, and I'm closed on Sundays, so maybe we can get together one of those days."

Bethany nodded as she rejoined David, who'd found a book to thumb through while she chatted with Denise. He looked up and winked when he saw her.

As they left, Denise waved and repeated. "Don't forget to call me."

They'd taken about ten steps when David turned to Bethany and stopped. She slowed down, and when it was obvious he wasn't going anywhere, she stopped as well.

Bethany turned and looked at David. He took a step back and leaned on the brick wall of the store behind him. "Are you okay, Bethany?"

"Yes, of course," she said. "Why?"

"I thought you were about to go into shock when you first saw Denise. Your face was white as a sheet." He didn't budge from his spot against the wall.

Bethany shrugged. "I was surprised, that's all."

"Surprised?"

Nodding, Bethany replied, "Denise was the last person I would have figured to own her own store."

"Why's that?" he asked.

Bethany chuckled. "Let's just say that we were wild and didn't exactly lead the lives of responsible kids."

"Who does?" he asked as he pulled away from the wall and started walking again, but not in the direction of his car.

She had to skip a couple of times to catch up with him. "I don't know. I just figured that certain people were destined to be better adults than others."

"And who makes these decisions?"

Bethany answered, "I figured things were pretty much spelled out from the beginning."

David shook his head. "Based on my experience, I've found that the least expected events are the most likely ones to happen."

She jerked her head around and looked him in the eye. "I don't know what you mean by that."

"Take Denise, for instance."

Nodding, Bethany agreed. "Yes, that's one of the least likely things I ever expected to happen. She worked in a bank, last I heard. In fact, I think it was a bank her father owned a piece of."

"I heard about that," David said. "It was on that corner over there, right?"

Bethany glanced up and saw that an antique and art gallery now inhabited the space where the bank used to be. She flinched. "What happened to the bank?"

"Denise's parents died, and the person who took over the bank made some bad investments."

Bethany gasped. "I never thought about things like that happening to banks. In fact, that one was an institution in this town." She'd heard about Denise's parents both dying a year apart, her father from a heart attack and her mother from cancer. She'd sent flowers to both funerals and sympathy cards to Denise, but she hadn't returned. Now she felt guilty.

He shook his head. "Like I've always said, nothing ever stays the same in this world."

"So what happened to the people who ran the bank?"

David shrugged. "Some left town and started fresh

somewhere else. A few of them opened other businesses with what capital they had left. A handful went to work for other companies that have come to the edge of town."

"How about Denise?" Bethany asked. "She was supposed to get quite an inheritance."

"She did," David replied. "At first she spent money like it was going out of style, but it didn't take long for her to realize she couldn't keep doing that."

"Sounds like she grew up after her parents died." Bethany felt sick about not being here for her childhood best friend.

Nodding, David said, "Yes, I'm sure. The woman we just left went through this about four years ago."

"But she looks so . . . so, well, I don't know, so happy." Bethany didn't detect a single note of bitterness in her friend's voice.

"She *is* happy, but that doesn't mean she always has been. In fact, when I met her, she was on the road to destruction." David turned toward a muffin shop and held the door without asking her if she wanted to go inside.

But she went in, anyway. She needed to sit down, after hearing that news.

"Nana used to say that Denise would self-destruct if she didn't change her ways." They'd found a table and sat down. Bethany put her elbows on the wooden tabletop and buried her face in her hands. "I still can't believe this."

"Like I said," he continued, "life is full of changes."

A waitress brought them some water, and David ordered a variety basket of muffins and coffee for both of them. "I hope you don't mind, but I have a weakness for the food here."

It actually sounded wonderful to Bethany. Although it

was nearly lunch time, she didn't feel that she could handle a heavy meal, after what she'd just learned.

"When did Denise become responsible?" Bethany asked.

He sipped his water, then put it back down on the table. "When I met Denise, she was working temporary jobs, and I happened to be new in town. I walked into a real estate office where she was filling in for the receptionist who was out on maternity leave. Since I wasn't sure what I wanted at the time, I told her I needed a rental house or apartment."

"So, did she find you a place to live?" Bethany asked. Even when Denise had been on a wild streak, she was always helpful to people in need. She had no doubt that her friend would have found David the perfect place to rent in a matter of hours.

"Not only that, she tried to fix me up with every eligible female in town."

Bethany laughed. That certainly sounded like Denise. "Did she find you a good one?"

He shook his head. "No, but it's not because she didn't try hard enough. I finally had to tell her to stop so I could get some work done."

"You still didn't tell me how she became responsible."

David paused and looked Bethany in the eye. "It didn't happen overnight."

Chapter Seven

Leaning forward, David steepled his hands over the table. "You see, it's like this. I knew that her job was temporary, and she was about to lose it soon. The agency that had placed her didn't have anywhere else to send her once it was over, so I decided it was time to get clerical help. I requested Denise, and she came to the church on assignment."

"Isn't that rather underhanded and sneaky?" Bethany said.

"Not really. I had quite a bit of correspondence that needed to go out. It was only a matter of time before I knew I needed to hire someone, so I figured I might as well go ahead and get a person with her skills."

Bethany nodded. One thing she remembered about Denise was the fact that she valued her fast typing and ten-key skills. "My dad wants me to have something to fall back on if I don't make it through college," she'd confided in Bethany. It seemed her father knew what he was talking about.

"So, was this a temporary job?" Bethany asked.

"At first, I thought it was," David said. "But after she got in the office and organized it, I felt like I couldn't do without her, so I got the church appropriations committee to approve her salary."

"But New Hope is a small church," Bethany said. "I don't see how they could afford a full-time pastor and a secretary."

Grinning, he said, "We may be small, but we're very generous."

"They must be." Bethany buttered another hot muffin and ate it while she contemplated everything they'd discussed.

"After Denise had everything like she wanted it, I could tell that she was getting antsy to do something else," David continued. "I figured she just needed to start her own business."

"Then I guess she didn't tell you about some of our escapades in high school," Bethany said, wondering how her friend had pulled the wool over David's seemingly all-seeing eyes. "We started all kinds of business back then."

David laughed. "She didn't have to. Everyone else in town felt that it was their duty to let me in on her past. But I didn't realize you were the friend and accomplice I kept hearing about."

"That's because Nana would have skinned them alive if they'd mentioned my name in the same breath with Denise's," Bethany said.

"So, that explains it," he said, still laughing.

Bethany was confused, now more than ever. Here she was, talking and laughing about her past with a preacher, and she didn't feel the shame that generally washed over her at the memories of some of the things she'd done.

Most of it was silly and childish, but she was certain of one thing, God wouldn't have approved of at least ninety percent of their pranks.

"But that doesn't explain how Denise came to open the bookstore," Bethany said after thinking through the whole thing.

"One day, someone came into the office and said that they'd been to Jackson and visited an upscale bookstore with comfortable seating and elegant music, and I noticed how that drew Denise's attention," he continued.

"How could she afford it? I'm sure that while the church was generous, there wasn't a lot of excess in her paycheck," Bethany said.

"No, you're right about that," he said. "But when her father died, he left her the money in a trust that had to go into an investment after she turned twenty-five."

"Her father was always very generous with his money," Bethany said, nodding.

"That's what I understand," David said

David paid for the muffins, and they left the shop. He guided her with his palm in the small of her back. She felt cozy next to David now, so she pulled away. Cozy was the last feeling she needed right now. Her main goal was to help Nana get back to her old self and then go looking for a job—somewhere besides Clearview.

"Have you got plans for dinner tonight?" David asked.

Bethany chewed on the inside of her cheek for a moment. She didn't have plans, but she also didn't need to spend so much time with this man. The comfort that she was beginning to feel with him was dangerous for her at the moment. She had to pull away and get back to her purpose.

Nodding, she lied. "Yes, I'm afraid so, David." She held her breath, hoping he wouldn't press for details.

He didn't push. "Then, maybe we can do something another evening. Jonathan wants you to join us soon at the Burger Barn."

Bethany couldn't help but smile. "The Burger Barn?"

He held the car door for her, and she slid in. "That's Jonathan's favorite restaurant. He considers that fine dining." He closed the door and ran around to his side. "Good thing for me, since I'm on a preacher's salary. He especially loves their chili-cheese dogs."

"I did, too, when I was a kid," Bethany said.

"Maybe you can be a kid again while you're here. We can go to the Burger Barn, then take a walk down to the park so Jonathan can work off some of his pent up energy."

Bethany couldn't get over how easily David seemed to adapt to having his nephew around. He was quite a guy to take on that kind of responsibility. After all, going from being a single man to having a small boy around couldn't have been easy. But he seemed thrilled to do it.

Bethany took in all the familiar and new sights as they rode back to the nursing home. Every once in a while, she felt choked up at a memory that flashed through her mind. David respected her need for silence. He seemed to have an uncanny ability to know when she didn't feel like talking.

"Well, here we are," he said.

Bethany held her hand on the doorknob, then turned to him. "Are you coming back in?"

"No, not today. I've got a few hospital visitations, then I promised Jonathan I'd spend the rest of the day with him."

"You're a good uncle," Bethany said as she opened the door.

"I try to be," he replied. "I know it's not easy for him,

what he's going through. I'm looking for diversions for him."

Bethany swayed as she remembered her grandparents doing the same thing for her. It was like déja vu. "Thanks, David. I enjoyed seeing Denise again."

"I'm sure she was thrilled to see you too. Denise is a live wire, and I can only imagine the two of you together when you were kids."

"Yeah," Bethany said. "You can only imagine."

He drove away laughing, but Bethany just stood there and watched him leave. David had no idea how wild and crazy she and Denise had been, or he wouldn't have been laughing so hard. He would have been praying for their souls, instead.

When she got to the reception desk, the woman at the counter motioned for her to come over to her. She tentatively stepped forward.

"Mr. Michaels wants to talk with you before you see your grandmother, Bethany." The woman smiled warmly.

"Is he in his office?"

"Last time I checked, he was. Why don't you go on back, and I'll buzz him to let him know you're on your way."

"Thanks, er . . ." Bethany couldn't finish her sentence because she couldn't remember the woman's name.

Mr. Michaels was standing outside his door when Bethany turned the corner to his office. He looked pleased about something. Hopefully, it was good news about Nana.

"Come in, Bethany," he said as he reached out and held the door for her. Once she stepped inside, he closed it behind her. "Have a seat."

She crossed the brightly lit, undecorated but functional

room, and took a seat in the chair across from his desk. Instead of going behind his desk, Mr. Michaels took the other chair on the same side. He crossed his ankle over his knee as soon as he sat down.

"So, how's it going, Bethany?" he asked.

"Uh, fine," she answered. What did he want to see her about?

He uncrossed his leg, then leaned forward. "I guess you know that I've been friends with your family for a very long time, and I have a special interest in your grandmother."

Bethany nodded. Nana had often said that her mother should have married this man, and if she had, they wouldn't have had to go through so much tribulation. He was kind and responsible.

"I want you to know that I'm doing everything I can to help your grandmother get well." He stood up, crossed the room, picked up a folder, and brought it back to show her. "This is your grandmother's chart. It has her entire health history listed, which doesn't really tell us much, since she avoided doctors and hospitals like the plague."

Bethany reached for the chart as he offered it to her. She opened it, but none of what it said made sense. She looked up at him for answers.

"Basically, Bethany, your grandmother's in good health. She has a little problem with blood sugar, but we've got that under control with diet. The stroke was a mild one, and we expect a full recovery in a few weeks."

"What can I do to help her?" Bethany asked him, sitting on the edge of her seat. There was obviously a reason he called her in for a private conference, and she had a feeling she'd only heard part of it.

"First of all, let her do a few things for herself. Keep reminding her of what day it is, since being confined often adds to the confusion after a trauma such as a stroke. That sort of thing."

"And?" she said. Bethany knew there was more.

He tilted his head forward and looked at her from beneath his heavy eyebrows. "Bethany, since you're her only living relative, I'd like very much for you to remain in town, even after she returns to her apartment."

"But I have to work," she argued.

Mr. Michaels folded his hands and continued. "It's come to my attention that you no longer have a job in Atlanta. There are plenty of job opportunities here in town, with all the new industry that has popped up since you left."

Bethany sank back in her seat. This wasn't what she wanted to hear. She'd never planned to stick around since she saw herself as a big city kind of woman. "I'll think about it, but I can't make any promises."

Mr. Michaels stood up and smiled, extending a hand to help her up. "Tell you what, Bethany, when you get ready to make a decision, I can introduce you to a few corporate executives in town who might need an accounting professional."

Taking his hand, she stood beside him. "Thank you. I'll let you know."

He stood at the door and held it for her. "Your mother was very proud of you, Bethany."

Bethany stopped in her tracks and stared at this man. She'd always considered him a distant acquaintance who was friends with her grandmother and an old flame of her mom's, but now she felt something different. It was almost like he knew her well, but she barely knew who he was. It was spooky.

She nodded and hurried down the hall to her grandmother's room. At least, there was good news—Nana would probably be just fine in a few weeks. But what Mr. Michaels was asking her to do was too much.

There were too many things to think about all of a sudden. Bethany only wanted to visit her grandmother, take a short break between jobs, and then start looking for work in a big city somewhere. Somewhere she could hide. Somewhere she could fall into a routine and no one would care whether or not she stayed alone. Here in Clearview, people tried to make things better, and sometimes that made her uncomfortable. They knew your business, and she didn't want herself exposed that much. She'd had enough of being in a small town where everyone had preconceived ideas of who she was.

After her parents' divorce, Bethany and her mother had moved to Clearview, where it was difficult for her to make friends in the beginning. However, one person, Denise Carson, made every effort to be nice to her.

Denise was popular, simply because she was friendly. Her father was a prominent businessman who made quick deals which resulted in a ton of money. But the money wasn't important to either of the girls. What was important was the fact that Denise had a man to talk to, someone who treated her like a princess. Bethany didn't have that, since her grandfather was quite old and died when she was a teenager.

Bethany finally got to Nana's room, which was all the way on the other side of the nursing home. At least, she was up in a wheelchair, so Bethany didn't have to lean over her in bed. She crossed the room and touched Nana's shoulder.

"Hi, there, sweetie," Nana said as she patted Bethany's hand.

"Hi, Nana," Bethany said as she leaned over and kissed the still-soft skin on her grandmother's wrinkled cheek. Then, she sat down on the edge of Nana's bed. "Are you crying, Nana?" she asked. The elderly woman's eyes were misty.

"Go on, child. Get me my hanky." Nana waved in the direction of the dresser. Obviously, she didn't want to talk about whatever was bothering her.

Bethany moved across the room and opened the top drawer. She pulled out a handkerchief and brought it to Nana.

"Have a seat and stop being so squirmy," Nana said, motioning to the chair in the corner of the room. "Let's have a nice chat, then I need to get some rest."

Bethany sat down and listened to her grandmother go on and on about things she wanted to do during the coming winter. She was definitely avoiding any discussion of her feelings.

Finally, Nana started looking around the room. "Where is my blanket? I can't seem to find anything anymore. How can I take a rest when I don't have a blanket to keep my legs warm?"

Bethany stood up and went over to her grandmother's bed. "Here it is, Nana."

"Good, child. Now run along so I can take a nap. I'll be up in an hour or two, and then maybe we can visit some more."

Bethany backed toward the door, feeling her heart in her throat. "Goodbye, Nana. I'll see you later. I hope you get some rest."

Then, she turned and almost started sobbing. Poor Nana looked so sad. The nurse spotted her and quickly came over. "She'll be okay. I've seen this type of thing many times, and it takes time. But Gertie Chalmers is going to be just fine. In fact, I'd be surprised if she wasn't back to her normal self in a week."

With a shaky smile, Bethany said, "Thanks for the encouragement. It's just so hard."

"Yes, I know it is," the nurse said.

Bethany's smile faded as she nodded. Then, she turned and got out of there as quickly as she could.

Mr. Michaels was standing at the reception desk as she got to the lobby. "How'd it go?" he asked.

Bethany was tempted to lie, but she couldn't. "She's depressed and a little confused, I think."

He walked her to the door as he told her, "Just keep visiting her, and you'll see the changes gradually happen. There's still some swelling in her brain, but we expect it to go down in a few days. By this time next week, she should be feeling almost like herself again—two weeks at the latest."

"I just wish I could feel as positive about this," Bethany said as she dabbed at her eyes with the tissue the nurse had handed her.

He scooted her out the front door. "Get some rest and come back tomorrow."

Nodding, Bethany did as she was told. She couldn't get out of there fast enough.

The second Bethany got to her rental car, she remembered that she really needed to return it. It was costing her by the day, and there was no point in paying the rental fee as long as her grandmother had a perfectly good car sitting in front of the apartment.

Getting the car back was no problem. She just needed to find a ride back to her grandmother's apartment. Who could she call? She felt like a stranger in town. She drove to the apartment and ran through the list of people who could meet her at the airport and give her a ride back.

Denise? Yeah, she could ask her for a lift, and she was sure she wouldn't be turned down. But it wasn't

Denise's day off, and she hated to impose. Besides, Bethany wanted to get reacquainted with her childhood best friend in a different setting.

Mr. Michaels? Bethany was sure he wouldn't mind. But what would she say in the car all the way back to town? No, she couldn't ask him.

Her mind ran through several more people, but there were valid reasons not to call each of them. Either it was asking too much, or they would ask too many questions. Bethany didn't feel like explaining anything to anyone right now.

The only logical person left to call was David, and that really bothered her. He'd been so kind already, but she didn't want to take advantage of him or owe him more than she already did. However, what choice did she have?

With only a moment of hesitation, she reached into her purse, took out his card, and looked at the phone number. She dialed the numbers and let the phone ring. After four rings, an answering machine picked up. Normally, she didn't leave messages, but she was desperate. She couldn't afford to keep the car much longer, so she had to find a ride soon.

After she left the message for him to return her call, she kicked off her heels and went back to the bedroom where she'd left her open suitcase with casual clothes. She pulled out a pair of blue jeans and a sweater and quickly changed into them. Right when she got the sweater over her head, the phone rang. It was David.

He sounded overjoyed at the prospect of driving her back from the airport. "Are you sure you don't mind? I know you're probably pretty busy, but I figured if we went first thing in the morning, you could get back to do whatever you have to do."

"Why don't we go ahead and do it now?" he asked.

"Now?" she said, her voice squeaking. "I don't think they're open this late."

He chuckled. "I just happen to know that they have electronic check-in so you can drop the keys in the deposit box. It's easy."

"Are you sure?" she asked.

"Absolutely. I'll meet you there in an hour."

"Thanks, David," Bethany said softly. He truly was a remarkable man, and she was extremely fortunate. She just hoped he didn't preach to her all the way back.

"Think nothing of it, Bethany," he said. "Jonathan will get a kick out of the airport. Maybe we can stick around for a few minutes so he can watch the planes."

She pulled on a pair of socks and shoved her feet into her sneakers. With friends like David, you didn't want to keep them waiting. Besides, now that she knew she'd be seeing him again, she had renewed energy.

Chapter Eight

Turning the rental car in was as easy as David had said it would be. He was sitting there at the entrance to the parking lot, waiting for her when she arrived. Jonathan flashed his snaggle-toothed grin, and her heart melted.

"Have you had dinner, Bethany?" David asked.

She slapped her palm on her forehead. "I forgot all about eating dinner. I bet I ruined your plans for the night, didn't I?"

"Only if you don't agree to go to the Burger Barn with us," David said with a conniving gleam in his eye.

Smiling, Bethany said, "Sounds good to me."

"I knew you'd eventually give in," David said. He turned to his nephew. "Lesson number one, Jonathan. Never let a woman turn you down for a date. Keep after her until she says yes."

Bethany turned to see Jonathan's reaction, and she caught his adorable giggle. She felt like reaching out and hugging him, but she figured that would embarrass him, so she didn't. Instead, she gave her own advice. "And be prepared to keep asking for a very long time, if you don't take no for an answer."

Jonathan burst into a fit of giggles. Bethany had a feeling that he had no earthly idea what they were talking about, but he was happy.

There was something really nice about riding in the front seat of David's car, with Jonathan sitting in the backseat. It felt warm and cozy, something she hadn't experienced in a long time. In fact, she couldn't remember ever feeling it as an adult.

"I hope you don't mind onions," David said. "We always order extra onions on our chili-cheese dogs, but I can hold back to the regular amount if the smell bothers you."

"What are you talking about?" Bethany said with a chuckle. "I want extra onions, too."

Next thing Bethany knew, she was involved in playing a street sign car game with David and Jonathan. Each time one of them spotted the next letter of the alphabet, they all cheered and then went on to the next letter. It was so normal feeling. And such a wonderful rush. Too bad it had to end.

"Well, here we are," David said as he pulled into the parking lot of the Burger Barn. "Wanna eat in the car or go inside?" he asked Jonathan. Bethany thought it was sweet that he was letting his nephew make the decision.

Jonathan put his finger on his chin as he frowned, concentrating on what he wanted. Then, his face lit up as he said, "Let's go inside."

"Good thinking, Jonathan," David said. Then, he turned to Bethany and winked.

Bethany couldn't help but grin back. David was wonderful with his nephew, a fact that meant more to her than all the money in the world.

While David went to the counter to place the order, Bethany and Jonathan found a booth in the non-smoking section. "I like to sit here so I can see everything that goes on," Jonathan explained.

Bethany sat across from Jonathan so she could study his features. He resembled his uncle, but he was still too young to tell if he'd have David's height, which was a little over six feet, if she was guessing correctly.

"Bethany," Jonathan asked, his face as serious as she'd ever seen it. "Do you have any children?"

Smiling back at him, she said, "No, Jonathan, I don't."

"Do you ever want any?"

She shrugged and closed her lips around her teeth but continued grinning. "Maybe someday."

Again, his face lit up like it often did when he had a bright idea. "I know what you can do. You and Uncle Dave can have a little boy, so I'll have someone to play with."

Bethany almost lost her breath at that comment. She found herself coughing to keep from choking. Unfortunately, David chose that time to bring the food to the table. "Are you all right, Bethany?"

She coughed again, and with tears stinging her eyes, she nodded. "I'm fine," she whispered hoarsely.

"What happened?" David asked as he turned to Jonathan.

Bethany held her breath, wondering what the little boy would say. "I just told her that I wanted someone to play with, and she started choking. Maybe she's got something stuck in her throat, Uncle Dave. Should we hit her on the back, or something?"

David winked at Bethany, then turned to Jonathan. "I

don't know, sport. Why don't we ask her?" He looked
at Bethany. "Want us to hit you on the back or something?"

Still unable to talk, Bethany shook her head. She
wasn't even sure if she'd be able to eat after that comment from Jonathan.

"She doesn't want us to, Jonathan, so we'd better eat
before the food gets cold."

Jonathan's excitement grew as David placed a huge
chili-cheese dog, a large order of fries, and a thick milk
shake in front of him. "Can he eat all that?" Bethany
asked, her eyes wide with amazement. "He's such a little
boy."

David nodded. "He's a growing boy, Bethany. He can
eat more than the two of us put together."

Jonathan puffed out his chest and pounded it with his
fists. "I might look little to you now, but I'm going to
be huge when I grow up." He said this in the deepest
voice he could manage and the result was comical.

Bethany had to stifle a giggle. "I'll just bet you will,
Jonathan. I can already tell you're well on your way."

David offered Bethany another wink, a gesture that
she was growing increasingly familiar with. It felt wonderful to share something like this with such a nice man.

"Hey, Uncle Dave, did you see that new dessert they
have now?" Jonathan had just bitten off a huge chunk
of his chili dog, and he hadn't finished chewing it yet.

"Don't talk with your mouth full, sport," David ad-
vised as naturally as Bethany had ever heard from a parent. She never ceased being amazed at his parenting
skills.

Jonathan finished chewing, then repeated his comment
about the dessert. "Can we get one?"

Shaking his head, David said, "Sure, Jonathan. But

you have to promise not to pop wide open in the car. It could get very messy."

Jonathan rolled his eyes and gave Bethany one of those I-can't-believe-he-said-that looks. Then, he let out an animated sigh. "If I mess up your car, I promise to clean it all up."

"In that case, I'll get you one," David said. He turned to Bethany, who knew she'd have a difficult time finishing the food she had already sitting in front of her. "How about you? Dessert?"

She raised her eyebrows and shook her head. "I can't make the same promise Jonathan made. I just know I'd pop."

"Girls," Jonathan said. "They're all a bunch of wimps."

David chuckled as he shoved the last of his chili dog into his mouth. He chewed it quickly and swallowed. "You can say that again." Then, he stood up to go order dessert for himself and Jonathan.

"You can have a bite of mine if you want one," Jonathan offered. "My dad always said that girls don't want to let guys see how much they can really eat, but I promise I won't tell anyone if you want more."

Bethany had to laugh. This little boy was so refreshingly honest. Too bad grown-ups couldn't be like that.

"When you were a kid, what did you like to do?" he asked, looking serious with his arms folded and resting on the table in front of him.

"Well, let's see," she began. "I used to roller skate, ride my bike, and climb a tree in your Uncle Dave's back yard."

His eyes widened. "Really? You knew someone who used to live there?"

Bethany nodded and smiled at his openness. "Yes, I did. In fact, I used to live in that house."

"You did?"

"Yes, I sure did. I lived there with my mom, my grandmother, and my grandfather."

"How about your daddy? Did he live there, too?" Jonathan asked, still innocent but touching on something that made Bethany wince. She didn't want to have to go into that part of her past, so she wasn't sure what to say.

"No, Jonathan, my daddy didn't live there with us." Hopefully, he wouldn't keep asking more questions.

"Oh," he said as he wrinkled his forehead. Bethany held her breath as he opened his mouth to ask another question. "Which tree did you climb?"

She let her breath out in a whoosh. She felt more relief than anything else. Then, she remembered the old oak tree, and her heart twisted. "The tree's not there anymore."

He cocked his head to one side. "What happened to it? Did the wind blow it down?"

"No," she said. "Someone cut it down."

"That's awful," Jonathan said, his face still wearing a deep frown. "Who would do something that bad?"

Bethany gulped. She wished she'd seen the direction this conversation was going so she could have diverted it. The last thing she wanted to do was bother Jonathan about something that didn't really concern him.

David arrived with the desserts. He plopped them down on the table and took his seat next to Jonathan, who was still sitting there thinking about the tree. "What's the matter, sport?" he asked.

Shaking his head in exasperation and picking up his fork to dig into his dessert, Jonathan said, "Some mean person cut down the tree that Bethany used to climb when she was a little girl. That's very bad."

The horrified look on David's face made Bethany cringe. What Jonathan said was the very last thing she'd expected. She was rendered speechless.

David held his fork about an inch from his mouth as he slowly turned his head toward Bethany, gave her a pained look, then turned back to his nephew. "Maybe the tree needed to be cut down, Jonathan. There might have been some problems with it."

His voice cracked, making Bethany's stomach churn. She wished she hadn't eaten that chili-cheese dog. Either that, or she should have kept her conversation with Jonathan on a less personal level. But how was she to know something like this would happen?

Jonathan appeared to think about it for a moment, then he turned to David and said, "I feel like climbing a tree, Uncle Dave. Can we go to that park with the big branches I can reach?"

David hesitated long enough to cast a glance over at Bethany before looking back at Jonathan again. "Sure, sport. But first, we have to take Bethany back to her grandmother's apartment."

Jonathan's forehead crinkled as he drew his eyebrows up. "Can't she go with us?"

With a forced casualness, David answered, "I don't think so. She has lots of things to do."

Bethany's heart dropped with a thud as she realized she wasn't being given a choice in the matter. In the course of one well-intended conversation, she had blown the opportunity to show her gratitude. Until now, she didn't realize how much it mattered to her. But now, she felt as though she'd lost one of the best friends she could have. And she'd only met him a couple of days ago.

As soon as Jonathan finished his dessert, they left the Burger Barn. Bethany noticed that after his first couple of bites, David didn't eat any more of his loaded hot fudge cake. It just sat there, the ice cream melting, the hot fudge dripping over the edge with whipped cream oozing over the sides, melding into one huge mess on his plate. She imagined that was how her insides were, all one big pile of mush.

Unlike before, David pulled up in front of Nana's apartment and let her out, taking off as soon as she was out of the car. She stood there and watched the back of the car, her heart and stomach ganging up on her, making her feel more miserable than she ever had before.

At least, she was familiar with the town. Bethany knew every single street, and she planned to drive around to see what changes had been made over the years since she'd been gone. It hadn't really been all that long, but it was long enough for plenty of new businesses to occupy the empty spaces she remembered. Another thing she needed to do was to stop by and visit with Denise. Maybe she could get to know her old friend and find out what had happened while she'd been gone.

Bethany forced herself to sit and watch television, something she'd never enjoyed before. After staring at the screen for over an hour, she remembered why. There was nothing worth watching. She finally pushed the "off" button on the remote control and headed for bed. At least she could lie there and read until her eyes grew heavy. That would make the next day come sooner, anyway, and that was what she wanted.

As soon as Bethany awoke, she hopped out of bed, made some coffee, and got dressed. The newspaper was waiting on the doorstep, which was a welcome sight. Maybe there would be something interesting that would give her some insight into the changes in Clearview. She read about many of the familiar names in town. Some things never change, she thought. The same people made the news now as before, and she enjoyed seeing what kinds of messes and trouble they'd found. Then, she scanned the ads. Hmm. Carson's Bookstore was having a sale. That was Denise's store. Bethany started her to-do list.

After visiting Nana, she planned to go to Carson's and maybe even buy something to support her friend. Then, she'd take a drive around town to get a better feel for the changes she'd already seen. She was amazed at the faster pace in Clearview, but it still wasn't as chaotic as Atlanta. Clearview still had that small town charm.

Bethany figured she'd go back to see Nana in the afternoon, then maybe spend a little time looking around at what she could do in the apartment. Mr. Michaels had assured her that if nothing else happened to Nana, she'd be returning home soon. Of course, Bethany would hang around for a few days or maybe even a week, then she'd have to get serious about looking for a job.

Bethany was getting tired of trying to figure everything out, especially David Hadaway, whose image kept slipping into her mind. He was the very reason she needed to stay single. Somehow, no matter what they did for a living, no matter what kind of people they were, men baffled Bethany. She finally rose, carried her mug to the sink, and finished getting ready for the day. It was time to get started.

The short drive to the nursing home at the front of the complex gave Bethany the opportunity to get used to Nana's car. It was big and old, but as her grandmother had always said, it was reliable. No sense in trading for a newer model when the older one suited you just fine.

Bethany chuckled at how Nana could be so frugal in one area yet so generous in another. She happened to know that Nana gave large amounts of money to her church, and she never scrimped on food or comforts in the home.

Bethany pulled into the parking lot and got out, wishing she could have changed the course of the conversation last night. Her heart still felt heavy.

She couldn't blame Jonathan for what he'd innocently said. He was just a small child who simplified everything in his mind. Because she enjoyed climbing the old oak tree, he thought that whoever cut it down was bad. There wasn't any gray area as far as he was concerned.

Suddenly, a light went off in Bethany's head. Wasn't that the very same thing she'd done when she'd met David? Hadn't she jumped all over the fact that he'd cut down something that had meant so much to her, when he'd tried to explain why he'd done it? Bethany had to talk to David. She had to apologize, not only for what had happened with Jonathan but for her own actions when she first came back to town. Now that her grandmother no longer lived there, it was none of her business what David did with his property.

She headed straight for Nana's room at the end of the hall. Hopefully, she'd see some improvement in her grandmother's health. When she got there, a nursing assistant looked up from the bed she was changing. "Looking for Mrs. Chalmers?"

Bethany nodded. "I thought I'd catch her before therapy."

The assistant glanced at her watch, then looked back at Bethany. "I think she's in the activities room."

"I don't want to interrupt anything," Bethany said.

"She won't mind," the nursing assistant said as she led Bethany toward the big room.

Nana's face lit up when she saw them. "Bethany," she said.

Bethany forced a smile. "Don't let me interrupt. Please continue," she said to the leader.

"We're almost finished," the woman said as she turned around and called another number for bingo. It only lasted another five minutes. Bethany wheeled her grandmother back to her room, listening to the older woman chatter all the way there.

"I can't believe how that woman can do all those things and get away with it," Nana said out of the blue.

"What?" Bethany asked, thinking she must have missed something.

"That woman, Blanche I think is her name. She keeps fooling around with all those married men. Seems someone would be on to her by now."

"Who's Blanche?" Bethany asked, now totally confused. Where did Nana get this information? The gossip grapevine must be alive and well in Clearview for the news to have made it into the nursing home.

Nana rolled her eyes and shook her head. "Don't you ever watch the soaps on television? Blanche is the town hussy who keeps stealing men away from their wives. And once she has them, she doesn't want them anymore. I swear. One of these days, she just might find herself at the wrong end of someone's fist. Personally, I wouldn't put up with that from anyone. If she so much as came within a foot of my man, I'd skin her alive." Bethany had to chuckle to herself. She could actually imagine Nana taking apart some woman, limb by limb, for doing something like what she was saying about this Blanche.

"I thought you were talking about someone you knew, Nana."

Nana looked at her like she was crazy. "Land sakes alive, girl. People don't do things like that in real life and get away with it. That's why I like the soaps so much. It makes me realize that my own problems aren't quite so bad. Those people make our worst citizen look like an angel."

Bethany laughed out loud this time. At least, Nana hadn't lost her sense of humor. That was one of the things she loved best about her grandmother.

They chatted for nearly an hour, until the nursing assistant came to get Nana for physical therapy. "Will you be back this afternoon, Susan?" Nana asked as she wheeled toward the door. She blushed, chuckled behind her handkerchief, then corrected herself. "I mean, Bethany."

Bethany hesitated for a second, then said, "Sure, Nana."

"Bring me a treat when you come back."

"A treat?" Bethany asked.

"Yes. Something good." She was already in the hall when she hollered over her shoulder, "Something chocolate."

Bethany left her grandmother's room laughing. Nana might have temporarily forgotten who she was, but there were some things she'd never forget. Chocolate had always been her weakness.

Before she left, Bethany stopped by the nurse's station and asked if it was okay for her to bring Nana a chocolate bar. The head nurse checked the chart, then hesitated for a moment. "Your grandmother's diabetic. See if you can find something with a sugar substitute."

Good thing she checked. Otherwise, she would have made a huge mistake and brought her something that could have seriously damaged the one living relative she had left. Hopefully, she'd be able to find something Nana would like without sugar. Otherwise, if her memory served her correctly, she'd have a tongue lashing like she hadn't had in a very long time.

Bethany headed for Nana's car with a purpose. She didn't see David until they almost collided.

Chapter Nine

Bethany jumped back a step. When she realized who it was, she smiled and a sense of peace washed over her.

David initially smiled back, but after a couple of seconds, the corners of his mouth turned downward. "Bethany," he said, nodding in recognition.

She was hurt by his lack of enthusiasm in seeing her. For the first time since she'd met him, he didn't seem to want to chat. He must be holding a grudge from last night.

"David." She reached out to touch his arm.

He winced and pulled back. "How's Mrs. Chalmers?"

Bethany narrowed her gaze. His tone was cool and aloof, something she wasn't used to with him. "Nana's just fine, David." She stood still and stared, trying hard to think of the right words to say, but she couldn't.

He forced a closed-mouth grin and nodded. "Nice seeing you, Bethany."

He walked away and was close to turning the corner when Bethany hollered out, "David! Wait."

David quickly turned around and faced her. He looked stunned, like a deer caught in headlights, but she couldn't let that get to her. She had to talk to him and set things straight, or she'd never have any peace of mind, especially since it was obviously still bothering him.

"David, can we talk for a few minutes?"

He looked around, then tilted his head, folded his arms, and widened his stance. The barrier he'd formed was solid. Bethany wasn't sure where to begin. "So, talk," he said in a different tone from any she'd ever heard him use.

"Uh, David, I can see that you're busy right now. Can we meet somewhere later?"

"I don't know, Bethany. I promised Jonathan I'd take him over to the new pizza place on the other side of town."

"W-would it be okay if I come to your house after he goes to bed?" Bethany asked, feeling like she had to get through to him, now more than ever.

David rolled his eyes upward, then looked her squarely in the eye. "That will be fine. But I can't stay up late. I've got a bunch of people visiting tomorrow from Atlanta."

"I don't need long. I'll be there at eight."

Bethany hoped he'd give her some sign of being happy she was coming over, but he just said, "See you then."

Her pace slowed considerably after that, to match her mood. Until now, Bethany didn't realize how important David's friendship was to her, but it was. His friendly, smiling face warmed her heart and gave her a reason to think about staying in Clearview. His cold stare did nothing more than to make her feel like she wasn't worthy of such friendship.

Bethany decided to head straight for Carson's Bookstore. Seeing Denise would be good for her now, especially after her less than pleasant encounter with David. Maybe her friend would have some insight to help her solve her problem.

The bell jingled as the door closed behind Bethany. Soft music played over the sound system, and the fresh scent of eucalyptus permeated the air. Denise had done an excellent job of creating atmosphere in her store. Bethany was proud of her.

"Bethany!" Denise shouted as soon as she looked up from the cash register. "I've been hoping you'd come by again soon." She rushed from behind the counter and grabbed Bethany by the shoulders, pulling her to her chest for a huge hug.

Then, she backed off a little. "You don't look so good. What's troubling you, bud?"

Bethany shrugged and bit her bottom lip to hold back the tears. "I've messed up something and I was hoping you'd know how to fix it."

Denise chuckled and shook her head as she placed her hands on her hips. "I've done more than my share of messing up, so maybe I can help you."

"Is there somewhere we can talk?" Bethany asked, looking around for a private corner.

"This is it for now, Bethany. I'm the only person working today, but I don't expect a big crowd. If you'll keep an eye on the front, I can grab a couple of mugs of tea from the back room."

"Sure." Bethany would have much preferred going somewhere more private, but at the moment, she had to take what she could get.

No one came into the store while Denise was gone, and Bethany was glad. Denise handed her the mug and leaned against the counter. "What's the problem, Bethany?"

Bethany took a deep breath, looked around, and let out a huge sigh. "I've made David mad."

"David?" Denise screeched. "David Hadaway, mad? This, I gotta see."

"Well, I did it."

Denise grabbed Bethany's hand and squeezed it. "You must have done a real doozy to make him mad. I've known him ever since he came to town, and I can't remember a single time when he lost his temper."

"No," Bethany quickly corrected her. "He didn't lose his temper. He's just giving me the silent treatment—the cold shoulder."

Rolling her eyes and clicking her tongue, Denise laughed. "That doesn't mean he's mad, Bethany. Don't you know anything about guys?"

"Wh-what do you mean?"

"They're all a bunch of babies. If they don't get their way, they make you suffer."

"But this is David we're talking about. Somehow, I didn't get the impression he was like most men." Bethany glanced down at the burgundy colored carpet. "I think I'm the one who's at fault, anyway."

"What did you do?"

"Remember that tree I used to love in Nana's backyard?" Bethany asked.

Denise nodded. "I thought you were so weird when you talked about that tree. Once you even told me you told it secrets."

Bethany chuckled. "Yeah, I did. At least I knew the secrets were safe." She cleared her throat. "When I first got back to town, I went straight to Nana's house . . . I mean David's house. And the tree was gone."

"Yeah, I heard the tree roots were cracking the foundation," Denise said. "David was worried sick about what your grandmother would do if he had to remove it."

On the edge of another sigh, Bethany went on. "I really let him have it when I first met him, and then he showed me the sapling he planted in its place."

"I'm sure David's not upset about that," Denise said.

"It didn't take long for me to realize he was right. He was very nice about it, even when I acted like a spoiled brat on that first day."

Denise set her mug on the glass top counter. "I'm sure he knows. Otherwise, having to cut it down wouldn't have bothered him so much."

Bethany went on. "Like I said, I got over it, and we seemed to be on the way to forming a nice friendship. But I blew it last night while we were having dinner at the Burger Barn."

"You had dinner with David at the Burger Barn?" Denise asked, her voice going up nearly an octave. "He must really, really like you—a lot."

"I'm afraid not anymore."

"What did you do?" Denise asked like a mother hen trying to get a child to confess.

"I made the mistake of telling his nephew, Jonathan, about the tree I used to climb."

"What's wrong with that?"

The memory of that night flooded Bethany, and she felt like she was reliving it, only in slow motion. "When he asked me what tree I climbed, I told him an old oak tree that was cut down." Then, she added, "I didn't hide the fact that I was sad about it."

Nodding, realization crossed Denise's face. "Now, I

get the picture. Jonathan's mad at David for cutting down your climbing tree."

"Something like that." Bethany placed her empty mug beside Denise's.

"You'll just have to give him some time to get over it."

"I'm going to his house tonight to try to straighten it out, and I was hoping you could help me."

Denise picked up both mugs by the handles. "I can't go with you, if that's what you want. I have plans."

"No, that's not what I wanted. I just wanted some advice as to how to deal with this."

"Give him time, like I said. Men process things differently from women. I've had to learn that the hard way." She began to walk toward the back room to return the mugs, then she stopped and continued. "Tell him you're sorry for how it sounded when you talked to Jonathan."

Bethany was left standing alone while Denise went to the back room. She glanced around the room filled with books, and she decided to check out a few. Denise startled her when she returned.

"I'm sure it'll all blow over, Bethany. David doesn't hold grudges," Denise said.

"I certainly hope not."

With her eyes narrowed, Denise added, "I think you like him a lot."

Bethany glanced toward the door so she could make a quick getaway. It was starting to get rather stuffy inside. "Well, I guess I'd better go. Got things to do."

Denise offered an understanding smile. "Come back any time you feel like it. You're always welcome."

Bethany got into her grandmother's old car and cruised around town, marveling at all the changes and how they actually enhanced the small town. It was nothing like what she'd expected, since so many people made progress out to look bad. In the case of Clearview, Bethany was pleased to admit, progress was like a breath of fresh air. The city leaders had obviously done careful planning, and it showed.

After a quick bite of lunch at one of the new fast-food restaurants on the edge of town, Bethany made her way back to Main Street. She needed to pick up some sugar-free chocolate candy for Nana before she went back for her afternoon visit.

If her memory served her correctly, the five and dime was *the* place to buy candy, with the biggest selection in town. She parked her car on the street, fed the meter, and went into the old store that looked the same as it always did.

"As you can see, we have everything else. But if you want the stuff without sugar, you'd better go to Tony's," the manager said apologetically. He was referring to the drug store on the corner that had been there since the town started.

"Thanks, Mr. Blackstock," Bethany said as she left the store. A warmth had washed over her when she realized there was some continuity in this changing town. Mr. Blackstock was the manager of the five and dime when she was a little girl, and it appeared that he hadn't aged a single bit. Must be the relaxing atmosphere of small town life, she figured.

Tony's Drug Store was only a block away, so she got there in a matter of minutes. The place was super organized, with all the shelves labeled and directional signs hanging from the ceiling. Even that hadn't changed.

Bethany found the sugar-free candy right away, but she was stunned by the huge selection. Fortunately, a young woman clad in the store uniform smock came up to her. "May I help you, ma'am?"

After Bethany explained the situation, the woman plucked a chocolate bar from the shelf and handed it to her. "This brand's good. If she can't read small print, she'll never know the difference."

Bethany paid for the candy bar and headed for the car. By the time she got back to the nursing home, it would be visiting time again, and she actually looked forward to seeing Nana, especially now that she had a treat for her. Hopefully, the flavor was close enough to the original sugar-filled chocolate that Nana wouldn't be able to tell the difference.

She arrived at the exact time the visiting hour began, so she was able to walk right in. Nana was sitting up in her chair, but her head was tilted to one side, and her eyes were closed.

"Nana," Bethany whispered. If her grandmother was asleep, she could leave and come back later, she figured.

But Nana's head popped right up. "Susan!" she said. "Did you remember my chocolate?"

"I'm Bethany."

"Oh, that's right," Nana said, a look of sadness crossing her face. "Sorry." She closed her eyes, then opened them and asked again, "Did you bring the chocolate?"

"I sure did, Nana," Bethany said as she tentatively held out the wrapped candy bar.

Nana grabbed it like a small child who'd been sugar starved for a month and tore into the wrapper. It only took her a second to get the paper off the end. She stuck the candy into her mouth and Bethany held her breath. If Nana had any idea it was sugar-free, there was no telling what she'd say or do.

Then, she let out a long moan of ecstasy. "This is so-o good, Bethany. I can't thank you enough."

Bethany's breath came out in a whoosh. What a relief! "I'm glad you like it, Nana."

"These people around here don't know what good food is. And ya wanna know something else?" She pulled Bethany to her and whispered. "They think it's okay to serve fruit for dessert. They won't get away with that as long as I'm around. You'll bring me some more sweets, won't you, Bethany?"

Bethany backed away a little and nodded. She hated to deceive her grandmother, but as long as Nana was eating something that tasted good but didn't cause a problem with her diabetes, she figured there was no harm.

They chatted for a few minutes. Nana went on and on about the news from Clearview, almost like she wanted to bring her up to date on everything since she'd left.

When the announcement came that there would be a bingo game in the recreation room, Nana blew Bethany a kiss. "They're giving out good prizes, and I don't want to miss out. Last week, my roommate won a brand new tube of lipstick, in the exact same shade I always wear— Revlon Cherries in the Snow." Then, she wheeled herself out of the room and down the hall, leaving Bethany in the room alone.

At least, the sugar-free candy didn't upset Nana, Bethany figured. And now that she'd been left alone, it was probably time to head back to the apartment and try to figure out what to say to David tonight.

First of all, though, she had to ask herself if she'd really forgiven David for cutting down the tree that had meant so much to her. If she hadn't, then she'd better start digging deep into her heart. It was time to let go of something that was merely a childhood memory.

Besides, what was it about a tree? There were millions, possibly billions or trillions of trees in this world. And Bethany had no doubt that the oak tree had indeed cracked the foundation of the house. How would she have felt if the house had crumbled because of the tree roots?

Bethany pondered and considered every possible angle of leaving the tree as it was versus doing what David felt he had to do, and she actually wound up breaking into laughter at the absurdity of the whole thing. It was just a tree, for heaven's sake. Get over it, she told herself.

Bethany felt like she had her feelings and thoughts under control now. She'd learn to accept that some change was inevitable, while other change could be avoided. And there were some things that were more important than others, so just accept that, too.

It wasn't long before Bethany's head ached from all the thinking, worrying, and reflecting, so she decided to lie down and take a nap before going to see David. She wanted to be rested when she apologized.

She woke up four hours later with a start. One glance at the clock told her that she barely had time to wash her face, change clothes, freshen her makeup, and brush her teeth before it was time to leave for David's.

Bethany arrived on David's doorstep at precisely 8:00. The front porch light was on, illuminating the wooden front porch decked out with wicker furniture. Nana had wrought iron rocking chairs, but the wicker actually did look nicer, she had to admit.

David appeared within seconds and invited her inside. "Jonathan's been asleep for about half an hour. He's worn out from all the fun we've been having." His lips were curled into a half smile, which made him even more handsome than she remembered. His day-old whisker growth gave him a manly appearance, which only enhanced his trademark plaid flannel shirt rolled up to the elbows. He had the look of a lumberjack. An extra manly one. She thought he might be a hunk, but Bethany wasn't sure it was okay to call a preacher a hunk.

She followed him to the kitchen, where fresh-baked smells hung in the air. "I made some oatmeal-raisin cookies," he said. "And I have a variety of teas, if you'd like." He paused as if contemplating whether or not to sit down, but he remained standing. "Or you may have milk."

"Tea is fine," she said. "Let me help."

Even though he was being nice, tension hung in the air, but Bethany hoped she'd be able to do something about that soon. After all, that was why she'd come. She wanted to clear the air. They soon sat down, each with a cup of herbal tea and a platter of cookies between them. Bethany had never known a man so comfortable drinking tea in china cups before. David reached for a cookie and began to munch on it.

"So," he said between bites. "What's on your mind, Bethany?"

She wasn't sure where to begin, so she decided to just dive right in. "I want to apologize for what happened with Jonathan. I had no idea he'd take the issue of the tree to heart."

"Jonathan takes everything to heart. He's a sensitive kid."

Bethany nodded. "Yes, I can tell. But when he asked me what I liked to do as a kid, I told him I used to climb a tree. One thing led to another, and he jumped to the conclusion that whoever cut the tree down was a bad person. I never told him it was you."

"No," David said softly. "But I did."

"You didn't have to do that."

David leaned forward and looked into Bethany's eyes. He was about to say something, and Bethany had a feeling it might be a lecture. But it wasn't. "Yes, I did have to do that. It was the right thing to do." Then, he leaned back in his chair and lifted his tea cup to his lips, letting her know that was all he had to say about it.

"David, I know this might not make much sense to you, but I need to explain my feelings," she began. He nodded, and she continued. "When I first realized that oak tree, my tree, was gone, I felt a stabbing sensation in my heart. My parents split up when I was a little girl, and I desperately wanted something that was solid, something I could count on. Obviously, my parents had let me down, especially my father, since I never saw him after we left. But that oak tree just stood there, big and strong, its arms open, waiting to take me in. When I climbed it, I felt like I was resting in the arms of something that would always be there."

David nodded. "I think I understand."

"You do?" she asked, hoping he wasn't just saying that.

"Yes, I do. We all have things we come to depend on, and sometimes it doesn't make sense to other people. Personally, I need to know that I've always got a place for my nephew, and that's one of the reasons I wanted this house."

It sounded like he truly did understand. But there was something else. "Have you ever had trouble forgiving?"

David went on. "I think we all have a problem with the forgiveness issue at one time or another."

Bethany could understand that. "I'll bet you have to preach that a lot."

"Mostly to myself," he said. Leaning back toward her, he continued. "I can be pretty hardheaded."

Laughing with him, Bethany said, "I doubt you're any harder headed than me."

"If we had a contest, I know I'd win," David said.

Bethany felt her heart soften just a little bit more. "Then, you'll forgive me?"

David reached out and held her hands in his. "Yes, Bethany, and I want you to forgive me for doing anything that might have upset you, including cutting your climbing tree down."

Bethany's gaze locked with David's, causing her heart to pound out of control. There was no denying her physical attraction to this man. This preacher. The last man in the world she should ever feel attracted to.

Chapter Ten

David looked at the woman sitting across the table from him. He couldn't believe how quickly she'd found a place in his heart. From the first time he'd seen her, he felt the physical attraction between them. It was strong.

Bethany wasn't the most beautiful woman in the traditional sense. No, in fact, by most people's standards, she was a little too thin, her nose was a little too upturned, and her eyes possibly too big for such a waiflike face. But *he* was attracted to her, probably because of her vulnerability and consideration for her only living relative.

The first thing he noticed about her was the fact that she cared enough about her grandmother to drop everything and come straight back to Clearview to make sure everything was okay. But when she saw that it wasn't, he knew she felt a sense of panic because there was no one else to lean on. Bethany felt alone in the world, and he could fully understand that feeling. He'd felt it once before, himself. Bethany's eyes remained focused. When she opened her mouth to speak, he held his breath, hoping they could begin fresh, with some of their earlier differences behind them.

"David," she said, her chin quivering, making his heart melt. "I forgive you, but it's really not anything you need to be forgiven for. After all, you were only trying to save this house."

He smiled at her. It took every ounce of strength he had not to pull her into his arms and cradle her. He wanted to hold her, to kiss her, and to let her know that he'd take care of her. But the last thing David needed to do was make promises he couldn't keep. He wasn't sure enough of himself yet to form any kind of lasting relationship with a woman. She'd already made it quite clear that she planned to leave town as soon as she could in good conscience.

They talked for the next hour, discussing everything from quirks in the old house to Nana's potential recovery. "We make no promises, Bethany," he found himself saying, "but the doctors seem to think she'll make a fairly quick recovery and be so close to her old self that you won't even know she had a stroke."

Shaking her head and letting out a soft sigh, she stood up. "I certainly hope they're right, David. I miss Nana and the way she used to be. It hurts when she gets confused, even for a moment."

"I have a feeling she'll be fine," David said as he stood and held his hand out to pull her to her feet. "Why don't you try to get some rest, so we can talk tomorrow?"

She stood up to leave, and he had to resist holding her once again. Those lips of hers looked so kissable, but he had to hold himself back. Right now, she wasn't in the right emotional state to handle another feeling. Maybe later. But maybe not, the other side of David said. The second she left, David stepped back and closed the front door. His heart ached for Bethany. He'd seen plenty of hurting people, and he always wanted to make things better for them. That was why he'd become a preacher.

Clearview wound up being the perfect place for David's ministry. The town was big enough for him to have a decent sized congregation yet small enough for him to get to know each and every one of them.

Denise Carson was the first person he'd actually felt he had any impact on. The woman was running as fast as she could toward total destruction. She'd recently lost her parents, and she didn't know what to do with herself He felt that he'd met her in the nick of time. They'd quickly become friends. There were never any romantic feelings between them, but they had a mutual respect.

Gertie Chalmers was another major influence in David's life. When he'd first begun negotiations with her on the house, she'd seen something in him that most people never bothered to notice. "You're a lonely boy, aren't you?" she'd asked him the first time they met. At first, he'd denied it, but after a while, he warmed up to her and told her how he hoped he'd meet some wonderful woman sometime in the future to share his life with. She hugged him and told him that he was a good boy and he'd do well as soon as he quit worrying so much about things. Just because he'd been educated in a seminary didn't mean he couldn't learn from an older woman who'd lived many more years than he had.

Gertie invited him over throughout the negotiations, and she never got rattled when problems came up. "It'll all turn out fine," she assured him.

Finally, when the deal was closed, David helped her move into the retirement apartment, and he visited her as often as he could. She began to attend his church, and they were more like relatives than seller and buyer of a house.

David heard Gertie talk of her granddaughter often, and he found himself wondering why Bethany rarely visited. "She's got some awful job that keeps her busy six days a week, and I reckon she needs her rest on the seventh day," Gertie explained.

As soon as David had the tea cups washed and the cookies put away, he went upstairs to bed. It had been a long and emotionally trying day. He needed to rest before the group from Atlanta arrived tomorrow.

David had always been good with youth, so whenever one of his friends from seminary needed a place for kids to stay, David always offered his house. This group was on its way to do some mission work in a tiny town in West Virginia where factories had closed and people were out of work. Houses there were in a state of disrepair, and many people couldn't afford to buy food. Churches from all over sent people to help them get back on their feet and figure out how to bring more industry to town.

The stairs were quiet as he took each step. He chuckled as he remembered the piercing squeaks that echoed through the house when he first bought the place. He could see how Bethany found solace in those sounds, but he still didn't like floors that made noise when you walked on them. That was the first of his many repairs.

David didn't need an alarm clock as long as he had Jonathan in the house. It felt like he'd just gone to sleep seconds ago when he felt that familiar bouncing on the foot of his bed.

"Uncle Dave, get up. I'm hungry."

He sat up and watched his energetic nephew bounce a few more times, then hit the floor with a thud. He swung his legs over the side, reached for his jeans, and stepped into them. "Let's go see what we can do in the kitchen," David said as the two of them walked downstairs hand in hand.

One thing David had learned to do at a very early age was cook. He'd always enjoyed home-cooked meals, and the only time he ever got to have that was when he visited his aunt on the other side of town. His mother was always too tired to cook since she worked hard in a factory, so most of the meals she prepared were from a box.

"I want muffins," Jonathan stated flatly. "And eggs with bacon."

That kid sure did have an appetite. He'd probably grow up to be a very big man. Height ran in the Hadaway family. David was a little over six feet tall, his brother was a couple inches taller, and even his dad was about six-foot-two.

"Milk or orange juice?" David asked.

"Both."

David prepared breakfast for the two of them, just like he did every morning since Jonathan's arrival. When he really thought about it, David realized that having Jonathan around was good for him. He provided the grounding David needed. Too bad he didn't have a woman to share his life with.

Bethany's image popped into his mind. He wondered what it would be like to wake up next to her every morning and have her join him and Jonathan at the breakfast table. No matter how hard he tried to banish that thought, her image was still etched on his brain. Better watch out, he warned himself, this is a dangerous situation.

"When are the kids coming?" Jonathan asked.

David laughed. Jonathan had overheard him talking to his friend, the pastor from the Atlanta church, and he'd assumed David meant children when he referred to the young adults as kids. "They should be here in about an hour, Jonathan."

"Do you think they'll want to roller blade or ride bikes?" Jonathan asked, his eyes wide with excitement.

David shrugged. "I don't know. Why don't you ask them? They'll only be here overnight, so you'd better ask quickly."

Jonathan ate his breakfast in record time, and he ran upstairs to get ready, leaving David to clean the kitchen all by himself. David didn't mind. Most of the time, they worked as a team. David wanted his nephew to know how to take care of himself, so he tried his best to teach him his way around the kitchen. That wasn't all the kid needed, but at least it was something.

As soon as he had everything put away, David went to his room to get ready. He showered, shaved, and dressed just in time to hear the doorbell ring. He parted the curtains and saw the van from the Atlanta church.

Jonathan beat him to the door. He stood there, holding it open, disappointment apparent on his face.

"Where are the kids?" he asked.

David smiled down at the little boy. "These *are* the kids." Then, he went outside, leaving Jonathan to deal with his disappointment by himself, something he'd have to learn to do sooner or later, anyway. At least, this wasn't a terribly traumatic situation. Based on what David knew about this youth group, they still enjoyed many of the same things Jonathan liked.

He was right. As soon as the group was settled, he

was able to leave Jonathan in their care, and they already had plans to roller blade all over the neighborhood.

"Just make sure you keep an eye on him at all times," David reminded the leader as he backed his car out of the driveway. He needed to do his nursing home and hospital visitations, then come back and feed the pack.

The first thing David spotted was Gertie Chalmers's old land yacht parked in the visitors' parking lot. He smiled as he mentally pictured Bethany driving the car Gertie had insisted on keeping. There was nothing wrong with the car, but it was the least stylish thing on the road in Clearview, and easily the oldest car in town without antique status. He suspected it wouldn't be long before it, too, would be in the annual parade behind the '57 Chevy Brigade.

David's first stop was to see the administrator, Mr. Michaels, who greeted him with a hearty handshake and a big grin "Looks like you must have just heard some good news," David said. He had to pull his hand back quickly and massage it, Mr. Michaels had shaken it so hard.

"The best news in the world, considering everything else that's been going on." He stepped to the side and motioned David into his office.

"So, tell me about it."

"Gertie Chalmers just walked for the first time since the stroke. Bethany's in her room, and I can't get the two of them apart. Gertie skipped her physical therapy today because she's so exhausted from walking all over the place last night."

David's heart sang. "Hey, that is good news. I was going to stop by to see her, but if she wants to be alone with Bethany, maybe I'd better wait until another time."

"No, no," Mr. Michaels said. "I think they want to see you."

David stood. "Are you sure? I really don't want to intrude."

"I'm positive. Why don't you head on back there right now. I don't have anyone else for you to visit, other than the regulars."

David felt light on his feet as he walked back to Gertie's room. He heard sounds of their laughter as he got closer, and it made him feel wonderful to know that Bethany finally had her grandmother back.

"Nana, I can't believe you're still watching those soap operas," he heard Bethany say right before he turned the corner and knocked on the door.

Both women looked up and smiled when they saw his face. Gertie motioned for him to join them. "Is this a private party or could you stand to include another person?" David said before he took another step forward.

Gertie winked at her granddaughter. "Look, Bethany, it's the preacher boy."

David chuckled. One of the new members from the church had called him that, and the nickname stuck— preacher boy—now, if that didn't beat all.

"Okay, Gertie, don't fill her head with something else to call me. I'm sure she can think of enough stuff on her own."

Bethany's eyes twinkled. David could tell that she was trying hard not to laugh, but she wound up erupting in a fit of giggles. "Preacher boy?"

Gertie patted her on the arm. "Be careful what you call him. I think he's sensitive."

This time, David joined Bethany in laughter, and soon Gertie chimed in. As soon as he caught his breath, he bent over and gave Gertie a hug. "I'm glad to have you back." He loved seeing the joy return to her face.

She looked up at him with a puzzled expression. "I've been here all along, David. Where have you been?"

David felt Bethany's gaze, and he looked at her and winked. It was a moment to celebrate, having Gertie laughing and kidding around like she used to. He had to admit, over the past week, when she looked at him in sadness and fear, he was at a loss for words.

"I hear you skipped physical therapy today, Gertie," David said, pretending to reprimand her.

She shrugged. "When I woke up, my muscles were so sore, I couldn't stand up. Then, I saw my darling little granddaughter standing over me, and I didn't want to leave. You wouldn't expect me to be rude, now would you?"

"No," he said, chuckling. "Of course not. But tomorrow, you have no choice. You have to get back to work so you can move back to your apartment."

"Now, why would I want to go and do that?" she asked. "I like having my meals brought to me. And the prizes are better at bingo over here than they are at the clubhouse."

David rolled his eyes. "Why don't you get on the prize committee and do something about that?"

Nodding and clicking her tongue, Gertie answered, "I just might have to do that."

Bethany looked at David and asked, "How's Jonathan doing?"

Gertie groaned. "Oh, no, don't tell me you have Jonathan again. Did they split up again?"

David nodded. "They sure did."

"I hope they come to their senses, for the boy's sake."

"Me, too. But in the meantime, I have him."

"Jonathan's such a cute kid. He'll be all right if he stays with you. Don't let them bounce him back and forth like a rubber ball. It won't do him a bit of good, and your heart will be broken if something happens to him."

"I'm working on it," David said, hoping to end this discussion. He'd shared his personal life with Gertie, but he didn't think Bethany was ready to hear any of it yet. He looked up at Bethany. "Would you like to come to church on Sunday?"

He watched Bethany as she uncomfortably shifted her weight from one foot to the other. Obviously, she wasn't ready to attend the New Hope services quite yet. He knew that she hadn't stepped foot inside a church since she'd left Clearview.

"Tell you what, Bethany," he amended. "Why don't you come here at one o'clock on Sunday afternoon and attend services with your grandmother?"

Gertie looked up at Bethany with a pleading expression. "Will you do that for me?"

She'd been put on the spot, and David knew that she wouldn't disappoint her grandmother. She nodded. "Of course, I will," she finally said.

David couldn't help but wonder if Bethany felt like they'd ganged up on her. He knew that he hadn't done anything wrong. However, she might see things differently.

He spent a few more minutes chatting with the two women before he stood up and headed for the door. "Well, ladies, gotta run."

Gertie looked up at him and batted her eyelashes. "Must you leave so soon? Seems like you just got here."

Leaning over her wheelchair, he gave her a quick hug.

"Afraid so, Gertie. There are still some people who think I might know something important."

Gertie flipped her wrist playfully and said, "You know much more than I did at your age. Go ahead, David. Do what you have to do." Right in front of him, she turned to her granddaughter and said, "He's the best preacher I've ever heard, and I've heard quite a few in my day."

David laughed all the way out of the room. She once told him that at her age, she felt that she'd earned the right to say whatever was on her mind. And she did, too.

Chapter Eleven

"That boy's sweet on you, you know," Nana said as soon as she knew he was out of hearing distance.

Bethany stood up and turned her back to her grandmother. "I don't see how you can say that, Nana. We just met a few days ago."

"Mark my word, girl. I can tell. It won't be long before he lets you know himself."

It sounded strange, hearing that from Nana. Bethany couldn't remember her ever even hinting that a boy was interested in her.

"Bethany, I know what you're thinking," Nana said, dragging Bethany from her thoughts.

She turned around and faced Nana. "I-I'm not really thinking about anything."

"Yes you are, girl, and I think it's high time you got over your fear of getting involved. It doesn't have to be the preacher boy, but you need to relax and let some nice man get to know you. You've got a lot to offer the right person."

Bethany smiled at her grandmother. She meant well. It was just that getting involved with a man meant letting someone inside her heart. She wasn't ready for that yet.

"Thanks, Nana." She also didn't want to argue with her grandmother.

"Well, it's time for me to get moving." Nana began to push on the big wheels at the back of her chair. "I've got to work on getting myself back into shape so I can get outa here."

"That's right," Bethany agreed.

"Have you given much thought to finding a place to stay once I'm back in my apartment?" Nana asked, stopping long enough to look at Bethany. "You can hang around my place temporarily, but it's too small for both of us. Besides," she added with a chuckle, "I think it's illegal for you to stay there more than a month. Rules, you know."

Bethany nodded. "I know. I'm still trying to decide what to do."

"I heard about you quitting your job in Atlanta," Nana said softly. "You didn't have to do that on account of me."

"I know, Nana, but I wanted to quit, anyway. It was time to move on." Smiling, Bethany backed out of the room. She wasn't in the mood for a lecture. "See you tomorrow, Nana. I have a few errands to run this afternoon." Then, after blowing a kiss, she took off. She was so close to breaking down, she knew better than to hang around much longer.

The first thing she did when she left the nursing home was stop by the newsstand she'd seen on the edge of town to get a paper from Atlanta and one from Nashville. Since Nana seemed to be doing better, maybe she'd better start looking for another job. Big cities had more opportunities for accountants than small towns. Then, she decided to stop by to see Denise. She needed the comfort her old friend provided, and she wanted to share the news that Nana could remember her now.

The woman behind the counter looked up at Bethany. She said that Denise had gone on a break and could be found at the muffin shop. Bethany thanked her and headed in that direction. Her mouth watered as she remembered the flavor of the muffins she'd had with David. In fact, it sounded like a good idea right now.

Denise was sitting in a booth at the back of the shop, some folders and brochures spread out in front of her. She glanced up and widened her eyes in surprise when she spotted Bethany. "Join me?"

Bethany sat down across from her and glanced at what Denise was looking at. Obviously, she was in the middle of ordering books for the store. "Looks like you have your work cut out for you," Bethany said.

Nodding, Denise agreed. "Yes, it's a lot of work, but I love every single minute of it." She studied Bethany for a moment and narrowed her eyes. "What gives?"

"Nana's walking now." Bethany couldn't help but smile when she delivered this news. She was so relieved.

Denise squealed. "That's wonderful! How much longer does she have to stay in the nursing home?"

"As soon as she gets her physical strength back, she can go home. In the meantime, I need to get on the stick and find a job."

Bethany watched as her friend placed a finger on her cheek and thought about her situation. Denise's eyes suddenly lit up. "I know someone who runs the human resources department at one of the new factories in town."

Shaking her head, Bethany said, "I don't think Clearview will have anything for me. Too small."

"You might be surprised at what we have now, Bethany. We've come a long way since you lived here."

"I don't know," Bethany said, still doubtful "The salaries in Atlanta are pretty good compared to what I remember are offered here, and there are always plenty of apartments in the big cities."

"You might have something there, Bethany, but your cost of living will be much lower here. You can probably buy your own house for what you'd pay for rent in Atlanta."

Bethany hadn't thought about that aspect. It was worth considering. And she couldn't forget what Mr. Michaels had said about Nana needing her, even after she returned to her apartment.

She glanced down at the brochures. A colorful one caught her eye, so she picked it up. There were pictures of cartoon characters gracing the covers of children's books. "Somehow, I still have a hard time picturing you owning your own business.

Denise chuckled. "Yeah, me too."

Bethany watched her friend flip through the brochure pages. It was obvious Denise was busy.

"I just wanted to tell you the good news about Nana." She stood beside the booth and began to back away. She needed to start looking for a job.

"Don't be a stranger," Denise said as Bethany turned and left.

Bethany decided not to make any more stops today. So, she headed straight for Nana's apartment. Once inside with her two newspapers, she kicked off her shoes and made herself a pot of coffee. Armed with a red pen and a notepad, Bethany sat down at the kitchen table and spread the classified sections of the newspapers out on the table. Each job that looked close to what she wanted, she circled. Then, she went back and jotted down the contact numbers on her pad. Once that was done, she did the hardest part—she picked up the telephone and placed calls to each of the businesses that needed accountants.

Bethany was qualified for most of the jobs listed, but each one had something that didn't appeal to her. Several of them offered salaries considerably lower than what she'd made on her last job, and she'd barely been able to survive in Atlanta on her income. A couple of them required extensive travel, which she didn't want. She preferred to come home every night and be surrounded by her own creature comforts. By the time she got to the end of her list, there were only two jobs that sounded promising. The problem was, they were conducting interviews immediately. Bethany wasn't ready to leave Clearview, since Nana was just now on the road to recovery.

With a huge sigh, she flopped over on the table, her head nesting in her arms. Why did everything have to be so complicated? Nothing in her life had ever been easy, and she'd had to fight for everything. Right now, she was dangerously low on money, and she knew she needed to find a job, but she still needed to stick around town to help Nana. What were her options?

Then, she remembered. David had met Denise while she was working on a temporary job. Maybe she could do that. Swallowing her pride, Bethany dialed the number to Denise's shop to find out which agency she'd worked for. Denise was happy to give her that information.

"The only problem is that I don't type very well," Bethany moaned.

"You don't have to type," Denise answered. "They

find all kinds of job listings for people with any skills at all. Who knows? They might even have something in accounting."

As soon as she got off the phone, Bethany placed a call to the agency, where a friendly woman answered and said, "We'd love for you to come in and fill out an application. There are jobs galore, and I'm sure we can find something for you this week, if you want it."

Bethany's heart lifted. Although she wasn't ready this week to go back to work, at least it was good to know there would be something. She made an appointment to fill out the application and interview with the agency for the next day. Then, she rolled up the newspapers and stuck them in the box she'd been using for recycling. Her day had been filled with way more than she was ready for, and it was barely early afternoon. Now what?

Her first thought was to go back to see Nana, but her grandmother needed to spend more time in therapy so she could get better. Then, she thought about going shopping, but with the small amount of cash she had, she figured she'd better steer clear of temptation to spend it all.

Maybe a little television. Picking up the remote, Bethany did a little channel surfing. Her choices were the local news station, soap operas, talk shows, or shopping channels. No, thanks. She hit the "off" button.

Then, the phone rang. Thinking that it might be someone from the nursing home, Bethany picked it up and held her breath. Hopefully, nothing had happened to Nana.

It was Denise. "Bethany, I'm so glad I caught you there. There's been an accident."

Bethany felt her throat swell with that familiar lump. "An accident? Nana?"

"No," Denise said. "Jonathan."

Bethany's hand flew to her mouth. "What happened?"

"I'm not sure. He's at the emergency room right now and they can't find David. I wondered if you had any idea where he might be."

"Have you tried the nursing home?"

"I've tried everywhere I can think of, Bethany. We've even sent someone out to the church."

"Is it serious?" Bethany asked. The thought of something happening to Jonathan made her throat constrict.

"I'm not sure."

Bethany took in a deep breath. "Tell you what. I'll stop by the hospital to see Jonathan, then I'll go looking for David."

"Good idea. In the meantime, I'll keep looking, and I'll leave a message at the nurse's desk in the emergency room if we locate him."

So much for nothing to do this afternoon, Bethany thought. She grabbed her purse and headed out the door. Nana's land yacht, fortunately, was dependable and fast, and she got to the hospital very quickly.

A small group of older teenagers was clustered together in the waiting room, all huddled, looking worried. She didn't recognize any of them, but then she wouldn't. She'd been away from Clearview for a long time.

"I'm here to see about Jonathan Hadaway," Bethany told the nurse.

One of the teenagers quickly looked up and came over to her. "Do you know David?" he asked.

Bethany nodded. "Are you with Jonathan?"

The boy nodded and told her how they were the youth group from Atlanta and that they'd been in charge of Jonathan while David ran a few errands. He'd told them he'd be back to do things with them by mid-afternoon.

"We left a note on the kitchen table."

"What happened?"

The boy shook his head. "We went roller blading, then we came back to the house for a snack. No one noticed that Jonathan was gone until someone asked where the bread was. We all ran outside just in time to see him fall from the tree next door."

"He was climbing the tree, and no one was there with him?" Bethany screeched.

The anguish on the boy's face spoke volumes about how distressed he was. "He disappeared so fast, we couldn't keep up with him."

Bethany learned that someone had called the emergency dispatch number, and the ambulance had arrived within three minutes. That was something that wasn't likely to have happened in Atlanta. The traffic slowed down all vehicles, including ambulances and fire trucks.

"We still don't know how serious it is," the boy said. "David left a couple of numbers of contact people, and we called them. They're all looking for him right now."

Denise must have been one of those contact people, Bethany thought. And they must be very good friends, David and Denise.

Bethany waited with the group for what seemed like forever. She hated the fact that none of the hospital staff was letting them know anything, but the nurse had told her they needed to talk to his guardian first. As difficult as it was, Bethany understood.

Three hours later, she heard the familiar sound of David's voice as he came rushing into the emergency room with Denise trailing behind. His face was white as a sheet. There was a strange man right behind him. Bethany squinted her eyes and that was when she saw his resemblance to David. He must be David's brother—Jonathan's dad.

Bethany sat back and watched as David led his brother up to the nurse's station, showed his identification, and was led down the hall and through the double doors. Denise watched them leave, then backed toward the waiting area, where all the teenagers and Bethany sat watching, hoping for some good news.

Finally, Bethany couldn't take not knowing any longer. She had to find out what was going on with David.

Denise looked at her with the saddest expression Bethany had ever seen. "This whole thing is a huge mess, and everyone's going to wind up blaming themselves."

"But why?" Bethany asked. "It isn't anyone's fault."

"You know about David's brother and sister-in-law, don't you?" Denise asked cautiously.

"Yes," Bethany said, nodding. "It's so sad for Jonathan."

"You can say that again. I had a heck of a time tracking David and his brother down."

"Where did you find him?" Bethany asked as soon as she got over the shock of Denise's biting comment.

"I called his sister-in-law, and she had to track them down."

"Where did she find them?"

Denise shrugged. "I'm not sure, but I think he found him at work."

Next thing Bethany knew, a distraught woman with tears streaming down her chalky white face came through the doors. She was accompanied by another, much older woman who looked like an older version of herself. The two of them went up to the nursing station, and they soon went through the same double doors David and his brother had gone through.

"Jonathan's mother?" Bethany whispered. Denise nodded.

About half an hour later, David came out to the waiting room with a look of exhausted relief on his face. He motioned everyone to crowd around him, so Bethany joined the group.

David held his hands up and said, "Jonathan's going to be just fine. He broke his arm and suffered a mild concussion, but he's awake now."

"Did you talk to him?" the boy who spoke with Bethany asked.

Nodding, David said, "Not only did I talk to him, I got an order for dinner. He wants me to get him a chili-cheese dog, hold the onions."

Bethany let out the breath she'd been holding. David cast a quick glance her way, then turned to Denise. After a brief and quiet discussion, David nodded to her and motioned for her to join him. She did as she was told.

"Go with me, Bethany. I won't be gone long."

"David," she said as she reached out and touched his arm, which was rock solid. A bolt of electricity jumped to her fingers, and she pulled away as quickly as she could. He just stood there and stared at her. Bethany's mouth was dry. She didn't know what to do.

Then, Denise came up from behind and nudged Bethany toward the door. "Y'all better hurry. Jonathan's hungry, and you know how difficult a hungry kid can be."

Bethany went with David to his car, where they got in and rode in silence for a few minutes, Finally, he spoke.

"I suppose you're wondering where I was."

"Yes, I guess I am."

He chewed on his lip, then adjusted the visor. "It's a very long story, Bethany, and I'm not sure you really want to hear all this."

"Try me." She turned and faced him, studying his profile, wondering why he was so different now. He seemed darker, less cheerful than she remembered him being last time they'd been together.

"Tell you what, Bethany. We'll get Jonathan's order, then I have some personal matters to attend to. I have a houseful of guests who need to be fed. They should be gone tomorrow. As soon as they leave, we can talk."

Bethany crinkled her forehead as she drew her eyebrows together. She didn't have to know everything now, but she wanted some answers. "At least tell me what's going on with your brother and why he's not in there with his son."

David pulled into the Burger Barn parking lot and stopped the car. Then, he turned and faced Bethany. After a moment's hesitation, he said, "My brother and his wife can't seem to get along anymore. I have no idea what happened between them because they used to be so in love. But ever since Jonathan came along, they fight like cat and dog. I suspect it's the pressure of another mouth to feed, and my sister-in-law had to quit her job to take care of the new baby. Now, she's having a hard time finding a job, and their lives are a big mess. My brother can't seem to get it through his thick head that there's another side to this."

"Have you tried talking to him?" she asked.

He nodded with a pained expression. "He told me it's none of my business what he does with his marriage and to keep my nose out of it. In the meantime, I still have their son who misses them both more than you can imagine."

Bethany sat there in stunned silence. This was all news to her. Shakily, she reached out and touched his arm. "I'm so sorry, David. I had no idea."

He nodded and pursed his lips together. "I'd better get Jonathan his food or he'll worry about me."

Chapter Twelve

Bethany waited in the car. She was still in a state of shock from all the events that had happened, and she wasn't sure how steady she'd be on her feet.

He was in the Burger Barn for about fifteen minutes. By the time he got back in the car, Bethany had managed to absorb her new knowledge and the fact that David's life wasn't as charmed as she thought it was. There were some serious problems in his family, and he was right in the middle of them, trying to help.

"Got the grub," David said as he tossed the sack of junk food in the back seat. "I sure hope it makes Jonathan feel better."

Forcing a smile, Bethany said, "I'm sure it will. I remember when I fell and banged up my knees when I was a kid. My grandfather searched all over town for licorice whips that I said I wanted. He finally found them, and that made me happy."

"I'm sure you probably felt better, too."

Bethany nodded. "Yes, I did. It's amazing how something like that can take your mind off your pain."

David cast her an understanding glance. "We all have our ways of dealing with things."

When they arrived back at the hospital, everyone had already been in to see Jonathan. "He's waiting for you, David," Denise said. "I don't see how the kid can think of his stomach with a goose egg on the side of his head like that."

"He's a Hadaway," David said as he raced back toward the double doors, the sack of food clenched tightly in his hand.

Denise sat down and patted the chair next to her. Bethany followed.

"Well?" Denise said when Bethany didn't say anything.

"Well, what?"

"Did you and David have a chance to talk much?"

Bethany shrugged. "Just a little."

"David's been trying to counsel his brother and sister-in-law as long as I've known him, but they're so wrapped up in their own lives they seem selfish to me."

Bethany looked out the window, then turned back to Denise and nodded. "Jonathan's the one who has to suffer the most."

Denise reached out and squeezed Bethany's hand. "Yeah, you're right."

Finally, Denise stood up and stretched. "Why don't you come to my house?" she asked.

"I don't want to bother you," Bethany said as she shifted uncomfortably. Actually, she wasn't sure she was up to a deep discussion. "Besides, I need to call and see how Nana's doing."

Denise reached out and grabbed Bethany's hand again, this time dragging her toward her car. "You can call the nursing home from my house. We need to talk."

"About what?" Bethany asked. She held her ground while her friend looked at her with sparkling eyes.

"It's been a long time since we talked. We've got a lot of catching up to do." Denise seized the opportunity when Bethany relaxed, and she dragged her the rest of the way to her car. "I'll bring you back later, after I fix you a nice hot meal."

Bethany sighed. It had been a long time since she'd had home cooking. In fact, she couldn't remember the last time she'd sat down to what she'd consider a square meal with real nutrition rather than just something to fill her up and keep her stomach from rumbling.

All the way to her house, Denise chattered nonstop. Bethany just sat there and smiled at some of the humorous comments her friend made. Denise had always had a wonderful sense of humor and quick wit. It was still with her, even though she'd obviously changed her outlook on life.

She pulled up in front of a small house with flowers planted across the front in neat rows, the lawn green and lush, like thick carpet. It was nothing like what Bethany had pictured.

Denise was one of those kids in high school who had everything handed to her. Her father felt it his privilege and obligation to pamper his daughter by giving her the keys to a brand new car, a credit card to buy all the clothes her heart desired, and anything else she could possibly want.

While this house was adorable and obviously well cared for, it didn't fit the extravagant lifestyle in which she'd been raised. The house she grew up in had a very showy presence from the front.

"Whaddya think?" Denise asked as she put her car into "park."

Bethany smiled genuinely at her friend. "It's very pretty."

"Not what you expected, huh?"

Shaking her head from side to side very slowly, Bethany admitted, "No, it isn't."

Denise turned to Bethany and studied her for a moment. "I've changed, Bethany."

"I can tell."

On the edge of a sigh, Denise continued without making a move to get out of her car. "All my life, I searched for something to bring me my next thrill, but nothing ever made me truly happy. I had everything I could possibly want, materialistically speaking, but once the newness wore off, I felt empty again. Then, I had to get back on that hunt for something else."

"I always thought you were happy," Bethany said, shocked at her friend's revelation. "You were always smiling and laughing."

"On the outside, maybe, but deep down, I was hurting."

"Really?" Bethany squeaked.

"Come on, let's go inside. I'm starving," Denise said as she made her first move to get out of the car. "We can talk while I cook."

Everything in Denise's house was in perfect order. Small, but neat and tidy. The total opposite of how she'd pictured her friend living.

"Have a seat at the kitchen table while I figure out what to fix."

Bethany looked around the kitchen with its freshly

painted cabinets, the countertops holding nothing but a few electrical appliances, and the floor a sparkling white linoleum. "Your house is really nice, Denise."

Denise stopped searching in the cupboard, turned around, and looked at Bethany with contentment written all over her face. "And I did it all by myself. No help from Daddy."

Bethany looked down. "That's nice." The Denise she once knew had grown up. But what about *her*? Bethany felt embarrassment well in her throat as she realized she was still searching for something external to make her happy. And she didn't have a house and a business to show for her efforts.

"Losing my parents hurt more than you can ever imagine," Denise said, her eyes dry but the pain in her expression telling Bethany everything she needed to know. "You've never seen such a party animal in your life as I was back then, especially after my parents died. Good thing David came along when he did."

"What did David do?"

"He listened to me." Denise looked directly at Bethany for a moment before she emphasized what she'd already said. "I mean, he *really* listened."

Nodding her head, Bethany said, "He *is* easy to talk to."

"Poor David." Denise chuckled. "He had to listen to me rant and rave about how awful my life was. But he was patient, and he let me get all my anger out of my system."

"David is very patient," Bethany agreed. "I've noticed that, too. When I got back to town, I went off about my oak tree and how much it had meant to me."

"What did he do?" Denise asked, laughing.

Shaking her head, Bethany said, "He invited me into

the house to take a look around. It was strange. Anyone else would have ordered me off the property. But not David."

Nodding, Denise said, "Sounds like the same David who rescued me from myself."

"I still can't believe you have a business."

"Me, neither. If you'd have told me three years ago that I'd own a business, let alone a bookstore, I would have said you'd lost your marbles." She pulled a couple of cans from the shelf, then moved to the freezer where she found some frozen meat. "But I can honestly say I've never been happier."

"I can tell," Bethany said truthfully. "I just wish some wonderful things would happen to me."

"They already have," Denise said as she spun around and faced Bethany.

"Yeah, like what?"

"Like meeting David, and having your grandmother standing up and walking."

"Well, that's about all. Don't forget, I have no job and no place to call home now."

Denise went through the motions of putting everything together in the skillet while she thawed the meat in the microwave. Then, she sat down across from Bethany at the tiny table. "The way I see it, Bethany, is you have a choice. You can either dwell on the negative, or you can look at the positive things and be thankful."

"But when you're right in the middle of it, it's hard to see the good things," Bethany argued. Sure, Denise had suffered, but she was a survivor.

Denise shrugged. "Everyone has their own problems. It's all about how you handle it."

Bethany knew that her friend was right. After all, here

was a person who not only lost both her parents, she had to completely change her lifestyle for survival.

Bethany was amazed at what a wonderful cook Denise was when the meal was set before her. Being independent really agreed with her.

David had to deal with his brother, Dallas, and sister-in-law, Mary. They seemed determined to blame each other for Jonathan's accident. David felt it his duty to show them how this kind of thing had nothing to do with either of them and that they really needed to get their act together for their precious child.

But first, he had to check Dallas into a hotel so Mary could stay at the house without feeling like she had to go into battle. No sense in inviting trouble.

As soon as he got Dallas situated in the hotel, he headed home. On the way, he saw that Bethany's car was still in the parking lot of the hospital, but he couldn't find her when he went back inside. Maybe someone had given her a ride home.

He got home and checked on his guests, David figured it was time to talk to Bethany. He felt awful that she saw him going through so much with his family. He was the pastor, the person who was supposed to be there for others. The biggest problem with that was having someone to share his own frustrations with. And heaven knows, he had plenty of them.

David tried several times to reach Bethany, but the phone kept ringing with no answer. Where could she be?

Finally, he decided to call Denise. She'd been at the hospital. Maybe she knew.

"Stop worrying, David," she said after she answered on the third ring. "Bethany's right here with me. I cooked dinner for her, and we've had a nice, long talk."

An overwhelming sense of relief flooded David. He had feelings for Bethany he'd been fighting. He wasn't sure how much longer he could keep his distance from her.

"Are you finished with her?" David asked.

"Why? Do you want her now?"

Man, do I ever, he thought. He knew that he wanted more from Bethany than she was ready to give. In the short time he'd known her, he knew that there was something special between them, and he suspected she felt it too. But he'd have to wait until she was ready to give of herself. That is, he thought, if she doesn't decide to leave town as soon as Gertie was able to go home.

"I'd like to see her, yes." David had to hold himself back in order not to sound too desperate.

"Then why don't you come over and get her? Her car's still at the hospital. You can take her back."

"Are you sure that's all right with Bethany?" David asked. He knew how forceful Denise could be, and he knew that she was taking matters in her own hands, making decisions for Bethany.

"Of course, it is."

"Ask her," David ordered as firmly as he could without sounding as desperate as he felt.

"Okay," she groaned. He heard the muffled chatter as she held her hand over the mouthpiece of the phone. Then, she came back and said, "Bethany said that'll be fine."

"I'll be right there."

He got off the phone, took a few swipes at his hair with the comb in front of the hall mirror, ran out the door, then hopped into his car. It felt strange to be so anxious to see a woman, almost like being a teenager all over again. All the way to Denise's house, David had to work on calming himself down. He told himself over and over that he didn't know Bethany well enough to get involved with her romantically.

Romantically? How had that thought popped into his head? That was when it hit David like a ton of bricks. He'd fallen in love with Bethany. There was something about her vulnerability, a sense of neediness that made him want to pull her into his arms and hold her, to let her know everything would be okay.

But why Bethany? He'd been around needy women before, Denise, for one. He'd never felt anything other than friendship with her. He loved Denise in more of a brotherly way, quite different from how he felt about Bethany. One thing David did know was the fact that love took time to grow. What he felt for Bethany was more of an infatuation. He needed to spend more time with her to know if anything permanent could possibly come of it.

The biggest obstacle he could see was that she had said time and again that she planned to leave town as soon as her grandmother was able to make it on her own. She never once seemed to consider sticking around to see if she could find a job in Clearview.

Maybe he could talk to her, to make her see how she might be able to find happiness in the town where she'd grown up. Her childhood had been sad without her father in her home, but there had been some good times for her too. He knew that for a fact. Denise used to talk to him for hours about some of the things she and her friends used to do. Now that he knew Bethany was one of her friends, he had something he could remind her of.

Denise's house was on the same side of town as David's. It was an older area that had been built when the railroad brought the first settlers to Clearview. Most of the new industry and subdivisions were on the other side, and a lot of people preferred to move over there. But not David. He enjoyed the soundness of the older homes, and he loved the charm of the house he'd bought. When Denise expressed an interest in owning her own place, David had just found out that one of the members of the church was expecting their third child. They needed to sell their tiny two-bedroom cottage so they could buy a bigger house.

He told Denise about the opportunity to find something she could afford without having to touch the money her father had left her. Together, they went to look at the house, and Denise had fallen in love with it right off the bat. She was able to overlook the curling linoleum and the stained carpet where babies had spit up.

One look at the place and she clapped her hands together saying, "I want it."

A month later, it was hers. David listened to Denise as she enthusiastically talked about all the improvements she was making. She took it one thing at a time, until she got the house just like she wanted. He had to admit, he was pleasantly surprised when she invited him over to show the results of her hard work, most of which she'd done herself.

"This is wonderful, Denise," he'd told her.

She hugged him, then stepped back, saying, "If you hadn't been so supportive of me, I never would have had the courage to take on such a big project. But I did what seemed right, and look, hard work really does pay off."

David noticed the bright red and yellow flowers as he pulled up in front of Denise's house. She was always one who loved splashy colors, and he was glad she had such a nice, big canvas to work with.

As soon as he got out of the car, the front door opened. Denise motioned for him to come inside.

His heart pounded with anticipation. David walked up the sidewalk, trying hard to contain his excitement over seeing Bethany, knowing how he felt about her. It was the first time he'd admitted his feelings to himself, and it felt liberating, but scary. She grinned up at him shyly from the sofa Denise had bought from a second-hand store and had refinished. Her house was dollhouse pretty, as he knew it would be.

Denise backed out of the room inconspicuously, and David found himself alone with Bethany. "Hi, David," she said. "I hope Jonathan's okay."

Nodding, he sat down in the chair across from her. "As far as I know, he's just fine."

A moment of awkward silence filled the room. David cleared his throat. "I understand you left your car at the hospital."

Bethany nodded and offered a shaky grin. "I'll have to imposition Denise and ask for a ride back."

"No need for that," he said quickly. "I'll take you."

His voice came out much louder than he expected, so he had to clear his throat to regain self-control. He'd never felt this way as an adult. It was like being sixteen all over again.

"Are you sure?" Bethany asked. "I'm sure Denise wouldn't mind giving me a ride."

Suddenly, Denise appeared, laughing. "Actually, I was hoping David would offer. I have a few things I need to do to get ready for tomorrow—orders to place and a few bookkeeping entries to make."

David thought they'd already discussed this when he'd called earlier. Denise was up to her tricks. Oh, well. He was here now. No sense getting mad. He held his hands out. "See? Everything worked out just fine."

Bethany's smile quickly faded as she glanced back and forth between David and Denise. She looked suspicious, but she didn't say anything. Instead, she just nodded, reached down and got her purse, and headed for the door.

"Thanks for dinner, Denise. I'd like to return the favor sometime, but since I'm only here for a little while, maybe I can take you out."

Denise practically shoved the two of them out the door. "Sounds good. Maybe next week."

David held the door for Bethany as she tentatively slid into the passenger seat. His heart went out to her. She'd been ambushed, and there was nothing she could do to stop it. Fortunately, both he and Denise were fond of her.

Bethany seemed as worried about something. He reached over and took her hand.

"What's wrong, Bethany?" he asked softly.

She looked at him, her eyes glistening with unfallen tears. "I can't believe you, David."

"What?" He'd never lied to her. What couldn't she believe?

With a slight shudder, Bethany said, "You just had one of the most awful scares you could possibly have, yet you seem worried about me. How do you do that?"

At least, they were talking. "Life is full of scares and challenges, Bethany. I'm just relieved that Jonathan wasn't hurt more seriously."

Bethany closed her eyes. He studied her profile, and he wished he could have just stopped the car to share what he knew. But he couldn't. He was right in the middle of traffic, light as it was in Clearview.

"Why don't I take you to my house, and you can meet my sister-in-law, Mary. I think you'd like her."

"She's at your house? What about your brother?"

David shrugged. "He's in a hotel."

"He's your brother. How can you make him stay in a hotel, while his wife stays at your house?"

"Because my brother upsets her and I thought it would be better for Jonathan to be with his mother."

"You're probably right," she agreed.

"I'd like to talk to you tonight, but it's hard while I'm driving."

"Okay," she said. "But I don't want to stay out too late. I need to visit Nana first thing in the morning, then I thought I'd start looking for a job."

"In Clearview?" David's heart skipped a beat at the prospect of her sticking around.

She nodded and shrugged. "I thought I'd find temporary work until Nana got on her feet. Then, I'm not sure what I'll do."

David smiled. At least, there was time for him to get to know Bethany better.

They pulled in front of the house, where David stopped the car. He got out and ran around to hold the door for Bethany, something he loved doing. Nothing made him happier than being a gentleman with the woman who flipped his heart over, even if she did worry him to death.

The lights in the house were still on downstairs. "Mary must be waiting up for me," he said.

He felt Bethany stiffen as he guided her toward the house. "Are you sure she won't mind? I don't want to make her uncomfortable."

With a smile, David answered, "I'm positive. You'll

like Mary. She's a very sweet woman who has only recently realized that she's worthy of respect."

Bethany was still confused by all that was happening. She didn't understand the relationship and what the problem was with David's brother.

Mary sat on the sofa, reading a book. She looked up and smiled as they entered the room. "David," she said softly. Then, she glanced at Bethany. "And this must be Bethany."

Chapter Thirteen

Bethany was startled. How did David's sister-in-law know her name?

David introduced them, then left the living room while he went to the kitchen for something to drink. Mary motioned for Bethany to sit down.

"I've heard some wonderful things about you, Bethany," Mary said serenely. "David has really enjoyed living in this house. I met your grandmother last time I was here."

Bethany had to clear her throat from the shock of hearing this woman talking so freely. "I grew up here," she finally managed to say.

Nodding, Mary said, "That's what David tells me."

David sure was taking long enough, Bethany thought. She shifted uncomfortably in her seat as Mary made small talk. What amazed Bethany was the fact that the woman didn't seem terribly distraught about her latest marital problem and her son being injured and in the hospital. She would have been a basket case.

146

A few minutes later, David returned, carrying a tray filled with a carafe of hot water, an assortment of tea bags, and some condiments. "I see the two of you have been chatting. Did Mary tell you about what she's planning?"

Mary shook her head before Bethany had a chance to answer. "I haven't gotten around to that yet."

David looked at Bethany, winked, then turned to Mary. "Then allow me." He sat down and motioned for them to help themselves to the tea. "I've talked Mary into moving to Clearview, so I could give her a hand with Jonathan. It's pretty obvious that Dallas isn't ready to admit any fault in this deal yet."

"Dallas is your brother," Bethany said for clarification.

"Yes, but Mary's the one who's willing to make the effort to be a good parent." David reached forward and picked up a tea bag and dropped it into a cup, then poured the steaming water over it.

"What about school?" Bethany asked. "Jonathan's old enough to be in school full time."

Mary nodded. "I know. That's why I'm moving to Clearview. I want some stability in my son's life. If it weren't for David, I don't know what I'd do." She chewed on her lip for a few seconds before adding, "I'm afraid it took this awful scare with Jonathan to make me realize what we're doing to him."

"At least you realize that, Mary," David said with sincerity.

"I'm just glad you talked some sense into me," she said affectionately.

David smiled affectionately at his sister-in-law. "If it weren't me, it would have been someone else."

Bethany gulped. In the most trying of times, David remained steadfast.

"At any rate, I'm moving here. Hopefully, I'll be able to find a job."

David nodded. "In the meantime, you're welcome to stay here, Mary. I think Jonathan would like that."

"I'm sure he would. I just don't want Dallas to get mad at you."

"I think I can handle that," David said softly.

Bethany had no doubt that David could handle anything, after what she'd just witnessed. Her opinion of this man had just shot straight up. Nothing seemed to keep him down for long. Not even when disaster was striking all around him, taking a direct hit on what he held near and dear to his heart.

After a few more minutes, Mary stood up, grabbed her book, and backed out of the room. "Nice meeting you, Bethany. I hope to see you again soon." Then, she left David and Bethany alone.

David sighed. "Nice lady. Smart, too. I'm glad she came to her senses before it was too late."

Bethany chuckled. "Sounds to me like you're a good counselor. Somehow, this reminds me of what you did for Denise."

David nodded in agreement. "Big difference, though. She's just one person, and a child isn't involved. It was much easier."

Now that Bethany knew more about David's family, she saw things completely differently. He wasn't the charmed man she once thought he was. He'd suffered greatly too, but he didn't let it get him down. On the other hand, she'd felt sorry for herself and dwelled on the negative.

"Is there anything else you'd like to know about me?" David asked. "Looks like this is the night for me to tell all."

He said this with a smile, so Bethany felt comfortable grinning back at him. "I still can't believe how untarnished you are, after all this."

Shaking his head, he said, "Believe me, I'm just as tarnished as the next person."

Bethany didn't believe him, but she didn't argue. David looked at her with an intensity that made her squirm. There was something in his eyes that she couldn't read. Something that made her want to cross the room and hold his face so she could get a better look. He stood up suddenly, and as he reached for her to help her up, she noticed a different expression on his face. "Well, time to head back to your car, Bethany. We both have a long day ahead of us tomorrow, and we need to get some rest."

They rode in silence to her car, where she got out and thanked him for the ride. He sat and watched as she unlocked her car door and got inside. Then, he followed her through the parking lot and onto the highway, leading to their two separate destinations. Bethany had a strange feeling in the pit of her stomach. The day had been full of surprises, so she knew that it was probably nerves. David was right. They both needed rest.

It took drinking two mugs of warm milk and almost an entire novel to help Bethany find sleep. And to top it off, it wasn't restful, not that she ever expected it to be. But she wanted to look like she felt good so Nana wouldn't worry about her. Nana had always been able to see straight through Bethany's eyes and into her soul.

When Bethany arrived at the nursing home the next morning, Nana was being fussed over by several nursing assistants who had to help her with her hair and get her ready for therapy. "Can you come back this afternoon, Bethany?" Nana asked. "I'd really like to chat with you."

"Sure," Bethany said as she bent over and kissed her grandmother on the cheek.

She let out a huge sigh as she ran to the parking lot and hopped in the car. She'd dropped off a copy of her résumé at the local print shop, so she decided to stop by and see if it was ready. It was time to start looking for work.

Not only was the résumé ready, the print shop manager asked to speak to her. "I was wondering if you'd be interested in doing a little bookkeeping on the side for me," he said. "I used to do it myself, but we've gotten so busy with all this new business in town, I don't have much time anymore."

At first, she was tempted to turn him down. After all, she was an accountant, and bookkeeping was pretty basic. Then, she decided to go ahead and accept, at least temporarily, with the warning that she planned to look for a full-time job once she knew when her grandmother could return home. With a smile, the manager said, "Wonderful, Bethany. I've known you since you were a child. I always knew you'd grow up and make something of yourself someday."

Bethany squinted. She didn't remember the short, slightly overweight, balding man. But since she'd been in town, she discovered there were quite a few people who knew who she was, though she didn't know them. They made arrangements for Bethany to come back the next day so she could get started with the freelance bookkeeping job. She took her résumé and started off down the street. Since she was so close to Denise's store, she decided to stop in.

By the time she left Carson's Bookstore, Denise had a second freelance bookkeeping job for her. "Business is picking up, and I don't have much time for ledger sheets," Denise complained. "Let me know how much you charge. I'll be glad to pay you just to have this out of my hair."

Denise had never been very good at math, so Bethany understood the problem, knowing that the bookstore records were probably in a major state of messiness. She left the store feeling relieved that at least she had some side work that would pad her account until she could actually leave and find a real job. Then, she went to the temporary agency and found out that they needed someone who could do some bookkeeping for them as well. Not only that, they asked her to come in once a week and do their payroll.

Of course, Bethany informed them that it was only temporary. The owner of the agency smiled and said that was fine. She got the feeling that the woman figured she might be in town longer than Bethany anticipated.

By the time she got back to Nana's apartment, Bethany was exhausted. She only had a few minutes to grab a quick bite for a late lunch, then she needed to get over to the nursing home so she could catch the last few minutes of the afternoon visiting hour. It had been a full day.

"You look whipped, girl," Nana exclaimed the instant she saw Bethany.

"I am rather tired, Nana." Then, she told her grandmother all about the freelance work she'd gotten while she was in town.

"Wonderful! Sounds like you've gone and gotten your own business. Have you thought about what you're gonna call it?" Nana looked at Bethany expectantly.

Bethany tilted her head to one side. Nana was right. She *was* in business for herself now. With three accounts, she had more than most people when they went off on their own.

"I-I don't know, Nana. I haven't really given it much thought. It all came as a surprise."

With a chuckle, Bethany's grandmother shook her head. "That's how it works sometimes. You've got a skill that's needed, and people are willing to pay you for it. Just make sure you charge enough to make it worth your time."

That night, when Bethany got back to Nana's apartment, she pulled out her calculator and crunched some numbers. She figured out how much she made by the hour in her last job, figured in the self-employment taxes and all the other expenses she'd have being on her own, and came up with an hourly amount that she'd charge. Based on what she knew about this town, she seriously doubted anyone would be willing to pay her that, but she figured it would be a way to weed out business that wasn't profitable.

To Bethany's surprise, the next day when she called the people who'd asked her to do the work, no one balked at the price. In fact, Denise sounded pleasantly surprised.

"I was afraid you'd mention some outrageous sum, and I'd have to back out," Denise said. "Do you mind if I tell some people from the church? I know a few other small business owners who need help."

Bethany hesitated for a moment before saying, "No, I guess that would be okay."

"Don't be surprised if you get more business than you can handle," Denise warned. "And don't be afraid to say no. Just don't say it to me."

Laughing, Bethany said, "Of course, I wouldn't turn you down. I couldn't."

"Atta girl. You know what's good for you."

They chatted for a few minutes, then Bethany had to get off the phone. Her head was spinning, and she didn't want to sound ungrateful.

When Sunday arrived, Bethany rose and took her time getting ready. Nana had asked her to come early and have lunch with her, so she decided to skip the morning visitation. She was extremely nervous because it had been so long since she'd been to church, and she'd agreed to go to the nursing home services.

To Bethany's surprise, there were quite a few visitors who attended. Families of residents and employees filled the recreational room, taking most of the seating that had been set up by the staff and volunteers. The music was provided by the woman who came in and entertained the residents on Tuesday afternoons.

"We'd better go ahead and find our spots early," Nana suggested. "The place fills up fast."

If it had been up to Bethany, they would have sat in the very back, but Nana had other ideas. She pointed to the front row and said, "Let's sit right there. I don't want to miss anything."

David arrived a few minutes before the services, and Bethany noticed that he wasn't dressed up in a suit. In fact, he wore casual khaki slacks and a ski sweater. She had to grip her brand-new Bible to keep from shaking, she was so nervous. To her surprise, David only nodded his acknowledgment of her presence. He didn't look at her with anything other than casual friendliness.

When it was over, Nana remained sitting there and fanning herself with the hanky she held in her hand. "He's one of the nicest boys I've ever known. You should give him more attention, Bethany. He likes you."

Bethany shrugged and tried to act like it didn't matter. But she wondered if Nana was right.

After everyone filed out of the recreational room, David hung around and chatted with some of the family members. Bethany stood by the door and watched him as he patiently answered questions and nodded, never losing the smile that brought people to his side.

That was when Bethany realized she was falling for David. She already knew she was attracted to him physically. But now, she felt something else. A closeness. An understanding. The desire to get to know him better.

She supposed the feeling should have made her feel good, but it frightened her instead. In the past, guys were nothing but trouble to Bethany, and she had already made up her mind to steer clear of the opposite sex when it came to a romantic relationship.

Bethany started to leave her spot by the door, but when she moved, David motioned for her to stay. "I want to talk to you before you leave," he said, his voice soft but loud enough for her to hear him from across the room.

The people he was talking to left a few minutes later. The second they were gone, he walked straight over to her. "I was hoping you wouldn't leave right away. I hear your business venture is doing well."

Bethany laughed. "I never intended for that to happen. I just spoke to a few people about my résumé and temporary work, and before I knew what was going on, I had my own accounts."

"Does this mean you'll stay in Clearview?" he asked, hopefulness written all over his face.

Until that moment, Bethany was denying any chance of staying in town once Nana's health improved. But now, with David looking at her like that, she wasn't sure. "I don't know."

He looked overjoyed. "At least, that's a start. You didn't say no."

They walked together to Nana's room, talking about the weather and how the town looked beautiful after the first snow. Anything but their feelings. Bethany wasn't ready to share her feelings with anyone just yet.

Nana was waiting for them in her room with a smile on her face. "I was hoping the two of you would get together. Now run along and find something fun to do."

Bethany went to her grandmother's side and placed her hand on her shoulder. "I thought I'd hang out here if you don't mind."

David nodded. "I've got a few things to do back at the church, then I have to talk to Dallas and Mary."

Nana snapped her head up and snorted. "Is Dallas giving his wife grief again?"

"Afraid so," David said. "This time, I have to keep them apart, at least until I can get through his thick head what this is doing to Jonathan."

"He needs to be turned inside out," Nana said. "Want my help?"

David sighed. "I could probably use it, Gertie, but I'm afraid I have to do this myself." He looked at Bethany and added, "Jonathan's been asking about you."

"How's he doing? Is he feeling any better after that fall?"

With a chuckle, David answered, "He's feeling a little too good. In fact, he wants you to teach him the right way to climb a tree so he doesn't fall next time."

Nana looked up at Bethany and shook her head. "Don't tell me you're already influencing that young boy toward mischief."

"I—" Bethany began to defend herself before David cut her off.

"Don't worry. I told him that it would be a long time before he did any tree climbing. In the meantime, he needs to rest until that bump on his head gets smaller."

"I should say so," Nana said, interjecting her opinion. "Tree climbing's a dangerous sport. Didn't I used to tell you that, Bethany?"

"Yes, Nana, you did."

"Well, gotta run," David said as he backed out the door. "See you tomorrow?"

Bethany wasn't sure who he was talking to, so she looked at Nana, who said, "He asked you a question, Bethany. Don't be rude."

"Uh, sure," Bethany finally answered.

As soon as he was gone, Nana shook her head. "Such a nice boy. Too bad he hasn't found the right girl yet. He'd make a wonderful husband to some lucky person who can see beyond the fact that his hair's a little too shaggy and his pants don't quite fit."

Bethany thought his pants fit just fine. And she didn't tell her grandmother about the times she thought about running her fingers through that hair of his. Nana wouldn't understand.

By the end of the next week, Bethany had three more accounts, and she was having to turn down others. She couldn't believe her services were in such demand, especially since she hadn't advertised a single bit. It had all come from word of mouth, thanks to her big-mouth friend, Denise.

Denise called her on Friday morning, just as she was about to leave for the nursing home. Mr. Michaels had told her that Nana was doing exceptionally well and that she might be able to return home in another month.

"Stop by for lunch today, Bethany," Denise said. "We need to talk."

Bethany agreed to have lunch with her friend, then she went to the nursing home. Nana was having the time of her life.

"Look what I won in bingo," Nana said, holding up a few trinkets she'd been guarding in her lap.

"That's great, Nana," Bethany said as she leaned over to kiss her. "Have you been doing your exercises like you're supposed to?"

"Of course, I have. I should be running by this time next week."

Bethany laughed. She was thrilled for her grandmother, but she felt a sadness at the prospect of having to leave Clearview. But she still needed to look for a job, something permanent. They spent the entire visiting hour chatting about the accounts Bethany had acquired, Nana's physical therapy, and the fact that Bethany had a lunch appointment with Denise.

"I used to think that girl would wind up a bum. Either that or married to one," Nana said. "But David became her friend. Look at that girl now."

Yeah, Bethany thought. Look at her now. She had to admit, she'd never seen Denise so happy.

The visiting hour ended, and Bethany had to leave. She kissed Nana on the cheek and headed out for Main Street. It was time to see Denise.

When Bethany arrived at Carson's Bookstore, Denise was ready and waiting for her by the door. Taking Bethany's arm, she pulled her outside, and said, "We're going to take a walk down memory lane." Then, she led the way around the corner, up two elm tree-lined streets, and over to the back door of what used to be Miss Bessie's Boarding House.

"Wha—?" Bethany said. She thought Miss Bessie died years ago.

"You're not going to believe this, but the boarding house and dinner kitchen has reopened." She winked. "Miss Bessie's daughter-in-law couldn't stay away."

The aroma of southern fried chicken, gravy, and fresh home-grown vegetables filled the back room where customers served themselves. An entire kitchen crew stood around the three stoves and wall-to-wall counters, getting things ready for the people.

"This is wonderful!" Bethany exclaimed. "I thought that when Miss Bessie died, there would never be another meal served here."

Denise shrugged. "No one ever dreamed this place would make a comeback, but it did. And it's just as good as ever."

They got their plates and filled them with a little bit of everything. And when they sat down to eat, Bethany savored every single bite that practically melted in her mouth.

"Save room for pecan pie," Denise said as she pushed her plate to the center of the table.

After they finished eating, Bethany stood up and almost had to sit back down. I'm stuffed," she said. "I couldn't eat another bite if my life depended on it."

Denise chuckled. "Good thing it doesn't."

They walked in silence all the way back to the bookstore. Funny how when Bethany first arrived in town, all she had thought about was getting away again. But the longer she stayed, the more she remembered the good times. And there had been some. The people in Clearview were probably the friendliest she'd ever seen. There weren't nearly as many cars on the road as there were in Atlanta, so she didn't have to sit, stuck at a traffic light, waiting for three or four turns to get through. And the place had charm, a southern heritage that brought a warmth to Bethany, flooding her emotions every time she went downtown and looked around. It hadn't changed much. But she had.

"Can you stick around for a few minutes?" Denise asked as they got to the bookstore.

"Sure."

Several customers were in the store shopping, while the clerk rang up sales at the cash register. It was obvious to Bethany that Denise's shop was successful. Clearview was the kind of town where people supported businesses run by their own people.

They chatted for a few minutes, then Bethany said that she needed to go. She had a few things to do before starting her temporary bookkeeping service.

A part of her still wanted to leave Clearview. There was still that side of her that thought she'd have to have to leave for business; in her mind, to make it big, you had to go to a big city. But then, there was something here that soothed her soul, when she allowed the feeling to touch her. It was a deep, seething nostalgia. All her accounts wanted her to start the very next week, so Bethany figured she'd better get rest over the weekend. As soon as Bethany visited Nana for the last time of the day, she went back to the apartment and tried to put thoughts of staying out of her mind.

Her outlook on life was slowly changing, and she could feel herself going through the new doorways of understanding as she realized how wonderful Clearview could be if given a chance. Lights kept coming on in her head, which brought a smile to her face. Bethany felt a closeness to Denise that she'd never felt before, even when they were kids and hanging out together, getting into all sorts of mischief.

Bethany had never been a serious trouble maker. But she had defied authority and gotten into a few messes. Nana had chuckled and clicked her tongue when Bethany's mother fussed and scolded. "Young girls sometimes have to test their wings, Susan," Nana had said. Nana was Bethany's lighthouse, always there during the stormy times of her life.

When the knock first came at the door, Bethany thought it was the wind. But it happened again, so she got up to answer it. It was David.

"I thought you might like to get out for a few minutes," he said.

Bethany had to think of something fast. "Uh, I was about to go visit Nana."

"Good," he said. "We'll go together. I'll drive."

Bethany nodded. "Let me get my purse." She didn't have any excuses.

On the way to the nursing home, Bethany felt the need to make conversation. "Where are Mary and Jonathan?"

The muscles in David's face tightened. "Dallas came back this morning."

This alarmed Bethany. "Aren't you worried?"

"Of course, but what can I do? Mary wants to see him, and he *is* Jonathan's father, after all."

"What if something happens?"

Slowly shaking his head, David replied, "I don't think anything will. He promised he'd be good."

Nana greeted them with open arms. She shooed David off. "You need to talk to all these other old folks and let me have my granddaughter to myself for a little while."

That afternoon, after David left, Bethany hung out in

Nana's apartment alone. She had hoped that David would want to do something with her, but she also understood that he had family problems that needed to be dealt with.

She still didn't hear from David the next couple of days, which bothered her immensely. Maybe Denise would know something. As soon as she found a stopping point in her work, Bethany took a walk over to the bookstore. Denise looked up and waved her fingers while she rang up a customer.

"Have you heard from David?" Bethany asked after the customer left.

"No," Denise said. "And that's unusual. Generally, he comes in here several times a week, but I haven't seen him at all since Sunday. I thought maybe you were keeping him busy."

With a frown, Bethany shook her head. "No, I haven't seen him either."

Denise told Bethany to wait there while she made a couple of phone calls. When she came back, she looked worried. "No one has seen or heard from David since Sunday. Something's up."

That was when Bethany remembered what David had said about his brother coming over to be with his wife and son. Something must have happened to keep him from his usual routine, and it must have been pretty important to have kept him away.

"I think I'll go over there and check things out," Bethany said. "I have a couple of hours before I need to get back to work."

"Sounds good." Denise's forehead was crinkled with concern. "Keep me posted. Let me know if there's anything I can do."

Bethany's car was parked behind the copy center, so she had to walk the two blocks and then around to the back of the building. She drove as fast as she dared through town.

Chapter Fourteen

W hen she got to David's house, she saw a strange car parked in the driveway. At first, she hesitated to make a move toward the house, but her curiosity got the best of her. Mary answered the door.

"Uh, did I come at a bad time?" Bethany asked. "I can leave and come back later."

Mary shook her head. "You really don't have to, Bethany. I'm trying to explain why I don't need to go with Dallas this time."

"What?" Bethany was confused. She should never have just come over here uninvited. She should have called first.

Mary leaned forward and whispered, "David's here trying to convince me he'll act like the husband and father he should be."

"But I thought you wanted this," Bethany said, confused. "Why don't you go?"

"Jonathan."

"Oh, I see." Bethany understood fully. No mother

wanted to keep leaving her son, especially in the face of something so traumatic.

"So I'm staying right here until Dallas agrees to move to Clearview," Mary stated flatly.

"I-I understand," Bethany said. She began to back away to leave. "I'd really better be going."

"No, don't leave," Mary said, reaching out and tugging Bethany's arm, pulling her further inside.

Just then, David and Dallas appeared in the hallway. David smiled, and Dallas glared.

"Bethany," David said softly as he walked toward her.

"Is this the woman who's keeping you up nights?" Dallas asked with a smirk.

David turned to his brother and patiently replied, "Dallas, this is Bethany. She grew up in this house with her grandparents and mother."

Dallas let his head fall back as he looked at her through the narrow slits of his eyes. Funny how he could have most of the same features as David yet look so different. "Lucky you," he said sarcastically.

She took a step back. "I-I'd better go," she repeated She looked at David's lips as they drooped back to the frown he wore when she'd first arrived. "Unless there's something you'd like for me to do now."

David glanced over his shoulder and openly glared at his brother. "I'll call you if I think of anything."

Bethany couldn't get out of there fast enough. She felt as though the weight of the world was coming down around her, but she still had the desire to see David. Right now, she couldn't. It was dangerous for her heart, and he had more pressing issues to deal with.

She went back to the copy center where she'd left off and quickly found her place. The system they'd been using was an old pre-computer method, and her first priority was to switch them over to something that could be done with ease and take about half the time. Then, maybe she'd feel better when it was time to move after she found a job in a larger city somewhere. After she finished working, Bethany stopped off at a deli and picked up a few things for dinner. She'd just unwrapped the food when the phone rang. It was David.

"Well, I finally talked some sense into my brother," he said, his voice raspy with some sort of emotion Bethany couldn't identify.

"Good," Bethany said. She figured that was what she was supposed to say, but after that, she was speechless.

"Yes," he said. "That's very good."

"Where's Jonathan?"

"He's right here with me. We figured it would be best if he just stayed here with me. His parents need a chance to work things out on their own."

Bethany's heart turned over. Jonathan was just a little boy who needed his parents. Both parents. At least he had David, but that still didn't make up for the loss of the people who meant the most to him in his young life.

"Can I do anything, David?" Bethany asked. She was sincere. She wanted to help him with his nephew more now than ever, since she had a better understanding of what was going on.

"Maybe you can spend a little bit of time with us guys," he suggested. "Jonathan needs to see a softer side of life than what I can show him."

Bethany smiled. David was right, and she was more than willing to spend time with them. "I'll be glad to."

Over the next six weeks, Bethany fell into the routine of spending a couple of evenings at David's house, helping with dinner, showing Jonathan some of the things she'd learned as a small child, like how to pop corn in the fireplace, and reading stories to him. Since David had every single children's Bible story book available, that was what she read.

The whole situation became very cozy, with the three of them spending time cocooning in the comfort of this old house they all loved. Jonathan flourished, David laughed a lot, and Bethany felt better and more secure than she ever had in her life. At least, as long as she put the future out of her mind.

Mr. Michaels had told her that Nana could go home after a month, but he recommended keeping her another two weeks. "Just for observation," he said. "We don't want to send her home prematurely and have something serious happen."

Bethany agreed. At least, she knew that Nana was being well taken care of. "I've been in her apartment longer than I'm supposed to," she said, crinkling her nose. "I promise I'll start looking for something tomorrow."

"Don't worry about it," he said. "As long as we don't get complaints, we'll look the other way." Bethany was thankful for his understanding. She hated sharing her money problems with anyone, although her financial picture was quickly starting to turn around, thanks to the freelance bookkeeping jobs.

Bethany and David developed the routine on Sundays of having Denise pick her up from the nursing home, then the two of them, Bethany and David, returning for the second sermon he delivered once a week. Then, they chatted with Nana for a few minutes before he returned her to the apartment. Most of the time, she spent Sunday evenings alone, so she could get ready for the next week.

Her bookkeeping service kept her very busy, but in between appointments and spending time with the people she cared about, Bethany managed to send her résumés to companies in the large cities in the south. She still felt that her future was better in a place bigger than Clearview, but she didn't think specifically about what would happen when someone eventually did call her.

Denise brought up the subject of her bookkeeping service a few times. "Have you figured out how you're doing with this, Bethany?" she asked.

Bethany shrugged. She'd kept her own books, and she was amazed at how well she'd done in such a short time. In fact, she'd been able to put away quite a hefty chunk of money into savings. She figured it would come in handy when it was time to move. But all she said in response to Denise's question was, "I'm doing okay." Actually, she was doing much better than okay.

Looking at her from over her cash register, Denise clicked her tongue. "It sure does cost a lot less to live in Clearview than any big city I've ever been to."

Denise was right. While she figured she'd eventually move away, Bethany thought she might have to find temporary housing once Nana returned to her apartment. Rent was much less in Clearview than Atlanta. In fact, she could rent an entire house for half of what her tiny one-bedroom apartment had cost. But she didn't say that. She was afraid Denise would start getting ideas about her hanging around rather than follow through with her plan.

Bethany had to admit, the thought of leaving this time made her stomach churn. She'd grown attached to Jonathan, and David still made her quiver when he was around. The feelings she had for him were partly physical, but her respect for him had deepened, and she had a feeling that she might be falling in love with him.

Nana was the first to say something. "That boy's sweet

on you, I'm tellin' ya, Bethany. Why don't you let him know how you feel?"

"What do you mean, Nana?" Bethany asked, unable to look her grandmother in the eye.

Nana puffed her cheeks, then blew like a whale. "I'm not blind, child. You and David are so much in love, you're making yourselves miserable."

"I'm perfectly happy." Bethany folded her arms across her chest. She had to guard her heart.

"You would be if you'd just let yourself feel something for a change. You can't keep hanging onto that notion that you can make a life for yourself on your own."

"I'm just fine, all by myself."

"Nonsense!" Nana barked. "You've filled that head of yours with all those numbers for so long that you can't see the forest for the trees."

Bethany had to laugh at that. Nana had a tendency to play with wise old sayings so they'd fit whatever point she was trying to make. And she was good at it too. But funny.

"All I can say is you'd better start thinking of matters of the heart before it's too late. Men like David Hadaway don't come along very often."

"I know, Nana," Bethany said softly. David was a remarkable man, one who would make some woman a terrific husband. But not her. She couldn't take a chance and let her heart be broken by a man.

On her way out of the nursing home that afternoon, Mr. Michaels caught up with her. "Things are looking good for your grandmother," he said.

"I'm happy with her progress," Bethany agreed.

"I think that she can go home this week, if nothing else comes up."

Bethany stopped. She felt a mixture of emotions. Of course, she was thrilled that her grandmother was doing well enough to go home, but that meant she'd need to find another place to stay. Nana had offered to let her stick around for a few weeks, but both of them knew the apartment was too small for two people.

"Let me know so I can get the place ready," Bethany said, forcing a smile.

"Why don't you go ahead and get started?" he said. "It might only be another day or two."

As soon as Bethany got back to the apartment, she took a long look around. Most of her things were stored in a spare room at David's house, thanks to his generosity. But she still had Nana's dining room packed with suitcases and boxes filled with personal things. She needed to start organizing everything right away.

But before she began to go through the boxes, Bethany placed a call to Denise. "I need to find something to rent pretty quickly."

"Why don't you stay with me until you find your own house?" Denise offered. "I have an extra bedroom, and it would be fun to have a housemate for a few weeks."

"Are you sure?" Bethany asked.

"Absolutely. You know me. I wouldn't have offered if I weren't sure."

Bethany sighed. As much as she hated to intrude, she needed the time to figure out what to do next. The last thing she needed was to make a lease commitment when she might get called for a job any day now. She'd just sent a whole batch of résumés off to Nashville from ads in the Sunday paper. Apparently, accountants were in short supply there, and it looked pretty promising. That thought made her sad, in spite of the fact that she needed something permanent. It was time to move on.

"Thanks," Bethany said.

"Why don't you start putting some things in the guest room tomorrow? That way, it won't be so hard when you have to leave."

They made arrangements for Bethany to get the key to Denise's house the next day. Then, Bethany got off the phone and began to sort through her things, stacking boxes to be transported first by the door.

When she got to the end of the boxes, she noticed something sitting in the corner of the dining room she hadn't seen before when she was too tired to notice. It was a wooden rocking chair, similar to the one in David's kitchen. In fact, the detailed carvings were so much like his, she was certain that he must have made the chair. Her heart flipped. Nana must have admired his, and he was the type to make her one, just out of kindness. Since she was finished with the majority of her sorting, she decided to try sitting in the chair. To her surprise, it was extremely comfortable, providing perfect lower back support. Bethany leaned her head back and wrapped her fingers around the arms of the chair. Beneath the right arm, she felt some deep scratches.

Worried that her boxes might have marred the chair, she found Nana's flashlight in the corner cabinet and squatted down on the floor to see if she could fix the damage. She wrinkled her forehead, and then her nose as she thought she recognized the scratches. No, couldn't be, she thought.

Her heart pounding nearly out of her chest, Bethany stood up and turned the chair on its side. There, on the wood beneath the arm of the hand-carved rocking chair, were her initials, etched beside the date she'd carved, fifteen years ago.

This rocking chair had been carved from the old oak

tree David had cut down from Nana's backyard! Bethany felt so lightheaded, she had to sit on the floor to keep from falling over. This was a piece of *her* tree.

As soon as Bethany regained her senses, she glanced up at the clock. Too late to call Nana or David. She'd have to wait until morning. She headed for bed, hoping to get some rest, since she had so much to do tomorrow. But after what she'd discovered, she couldn't go to sleep. There were too many questions she needed to have answered. Eventually, she found restless sleep. After her umpteenth crazy dream that made no sense whatsoever, she popped up and headed for the shower. She might as well go ahead and get ready for the day.

The first thing she did was head over to the nursing home. Nana would explain about the chair.

Mr. Michaels caught her at the reception desk. "Good news, Bethany. Your grandmother can go home tomorrow."

Bethany gulped. "That's wonderful news." Then, as soon as she could, she skipped down the hall to see Nana.

"What's got you in such a tizzy?" Nana asked.

"That rocking chair in your dining room," Bethany said breathlessly.

Nana nodded. "Yeah, what about it?"

"David made it, didn't he?"

"Why, yes, I believe he did. From the old oak tree. Why?"

Bethany flopped onto the corner of her grandmother's bed. "I had no idea that's what he'd done with my tree."

"Your tree?" Nana said, smiling slyly. "I suppose you could call it that." She took a deep breath before continuing. "When he asked if there was anything he could do for me, I told him I wanted a chair just like the one in his kitchen. And," she added, "I wanted the section of the tree where you'd carved your initials."

Bethany nodded. "So, he turned that section into the arm of the chair."

Nana nodded. "I tried to pay him, but he said to consider it a gift of appreciation for such a wonderful house."

That made Bethany shiver again. David was, indeed, a remarkable man. He really cared about other people and what was important to them. He'd proven that over and over, and Bethany found herself loving him even more.

"I get to go home tomorrow," Nana said, changing the subject. "I hope you don't mind."

Bethany leaned back and chuckled. "Of course, I don't mind. In fact, I'm as happy as you are."

"I doubt that," Nana said. "I've got so many things I want to do once I get home, I'll be busy for the next ten years."

"I'll help you." Then, Bethany decided to tell her grandmother about Denise's offer. "Denise said I could stay with her until I heard back on my last round of résumés."

"You're not still looking for a job in Atlanta, are you?"

"Well, no, Nashville this time. I found a bunch of openings in the Sunday paper last week, and I thought I'd give it a shot."

Nana tilted her head in confusion. "But I thought you had plenty to do right here in Clearview."

"That's only temporary."

Through squinted eyes, Nana glared at her, making her feel very uneasy, like she was under a microscope.

"Only if you want it to be temporary. You could make it permanent, you know."

Bethany sighed. She wasn't in the mood to argue with her grandmother. Instead, she said, "I'll think about it. Let's just concentrate on getting you home."

"I know I don't have much room, but will you stick around for a day or two to help me readjust?"

Nana's voice sounded scared, so Bethany nodded. "Of course, I will. You know I'll do anything you want me to."

"Then stay in Clearview."

Except that. Bethany feared that she'd already formed too many attachments in this town. But she didn't have a future here. Sure, there were more businesses than there were before, but she wanted a bigger opportunity. And she wanted to hide from the fact that she was afraid of relationships from her past. Yes, she'd finally admitted it to herself. Fear was what had driven her away the first time, and it was about to send her away again.

As soon as she could get away gracefully, Bethany headed back to the apartment. She wanted to check the answering machine she'd set up to see if she had any response to the résumés she'd sent.

The blinking light made her heart jump. She pushed the button and played back three messages from prospective employers, one from Denise, and one from David.

She called the people in Nashville back, and after discussing the details of the positions, she decided to interview for two of the jobs. Then, she called the airlines and made reservations to fly there and back in the same day. No sense in hanging around until she knew if she'd be living there.

Bethany had been to Nashville enough times to know

that it was big enough to hide in, yet close enough to get to Clearview in a day if she needed to. She'd sold her car before leaving Atlanta, so she'd have to get a new one, but she'd have to do that anyway. Once Nana returned, she'd need her car, and Bethany didn't want to have to rely on other people. Besides, she had enough money in her bank account from the bookkeeping service that she could pay cash for a decent second-hand car.

"You're what?" David asked when she called him to ask for a written recommendation.

"I've got a couple of job interviews in Nashville, and I figured they'd want references. You don't mind, do you?" Bethany wasn't sure what to expect from David, but not the shock he displayed when she'd asked him.

He sighed as the seconds ticked away. She was beginning to think he might refuse, and somehow, that didn't bother her. In fact, she felt a surprising sense of peace about it.

Finally, he said, "Well, if you feel that this is something you *have* to do, then, I don't want to stand in your way." He cleared his throat. "I'll have it ready and waiting in the church office by tomorrow morning."

Suddenly, Bethany's heard thudded. She'd gotten what she'd asked for. Why did she suddenly feel like she'd lost her best friend? What was going on with her? Wasn't this what she wanted?

After drinking a glass of water and repositioning herself so she wouldn't have to keep looking at the chair, she called Denise. She figured she'd need two recommendations, so she might as well have them in hand.

Denise wasn't as nice as David. "I thought you were going to stick around Clearview, Bethany. Have you lost your mind?"

"But I need a job," Bethany argued.

"Don't be ridiculous. You've got more work than you'll ever be able to handle. Why would you need a job when you've got your own successful business?"

Bethany sat there, stunned. She hadn't thought about the bookkeeping service as a "real" business. It was just something temporary to get her through the lean times while Nana recovered. "I didn't expect it to last," she finally answered. "I just figured I'd do temp work, then go out and get a job with a company where I can get ahead."

Denise didn't waste a second to let Bethany know what she thought. "How much further ahead can you get than owning the company?"

"You don't have to write a recommendation if you don't want to," Bethany said, feeling strangely like she didn't know what she was doing. It had all seemed so simple until now.

Denise paused for a second, then said, "Okay, I'll write you one. But I don't like doing it one single bit."

"Thank you, Denise."

Denise laughed, but somehow Bethany failed to see the humor. "Think nothing of it."

When she hung up the telephone, Bethany slumped in her chair. She should be happy, shouldn't she? Nana was doing well enough to come home, and she had some excellent prospects for employment. In fact, she knew that she could probably get either job she wanted, since she had the perfect education and experience for what they were asking.

But she felt awful. It was almost as if someone had ripped her heart from her chest and stomped on it.

The next morning, Bethany went to the church and picked up the envelope with her name on it. Then, she headed over to the bookstore, where Denise had left a letter with the clerk on duty. She glanced at them, saw that they were exactly what she needed, and headed to Nana's apartment with a heavy heart. She was leaving the next day for Nashville, but she didn't feel the excitement she'd anticipated when it came to this point. All she could think about was the fact that she was leaving Denise, Nana, and David, the man who'd stolen her heart, in spite of the fact that she'd resisted any kind of romantic relationship. Then, she thought about it some more. Logic had to take over at some moment of time, and that was when she'd feel better, right? David was the pastor of a church that had grown to the point of bursting at the seams, and he was just doing his job with her, making her feel better about things. His attention was more in line with duty. Wasn't it?

And Nana had done just fine without her before. Now that she was healthy again, she'd return to the way she was.

Then, there was Denise. What an amazing success story! The woman had completely turned herself around and was thriving on her business. Would that have happened if Bethany had hung around Clearview and not left her friend to do what she should have done? Whatever the case, Bethany still couldn't rid herself of the heaviness that choked her. She felt a tug at her heart, almost as if Clearview had some sort of hold on her, beckoning her to stay. But she couldn't.

Or could she? The more she thought about her bookkeeping service, the more she realized Denise was right. No one she'd signed up for the service seemed to be unhappy with what she'd provided. In fact, both the copy center owner and the coordinator for the temporary employment agency had expressed undying gratitude for the messes she'd straightened out. And to be perfectly honest, Bethany actually enjoyed the freedom she had from having her own business and having the authority to set her own pace. To top it off, she had more money than ever, something she knew was the result of lower living expenses than what she'd had in Atlanta.

Both of the jobs she'd been asked to interview for were upwardly mobile positions with top-notch companies. She'd be a fool not to go for either one of them. But Nashville was a long way from Nana. What if something happened?

Then again, Nashville offered more employment opportunities than Clearview. One of these positions could be what she was waiting for.

Her interviews were scheduled for the next day. Bethany had to scrape herself from her pit of despair and force herself to put on the professional image she'd worked so hard at perfecting. Even if her heart wasn't in it, it was just something she had to do.

That night should have been a restful one, but Bethany had a difficult time getting to sleep. She'd experienced sleepless nights before, but in recent weeks, she'd felt a sense of peace she'd never felt before. At least she'd be able to return tomorrow night with some idea of where she stood in the interviewing process.

Bethany rose early the next morning, showered, and dressed in her most conservative business suit. As she glanced in the full-length mirror, she saw that she hadn't lost the look, but she now felt different inside. She no longer felt the driving force that urged her to get ahead in the corporate world. What she saw was more like an actress who had the part of an executive, and when the director said, "Cut!" she'd be able to get back to the comfortable life she'd etched out since being back in Clearview.

Chapter Fifteen

"Looks like you're exactly what we've been looking for, Bethany," the accounting department manager said as he read over her recommendations from David and Denise. "Your credentials are perfect. Excellent references."

Bethany smiled back at him, trying hard to feel the excitement she would have felt months ago. But all she felt was an overwhelming sadness.

"When can you start?" he asked. "Of course, we have some preliminary things to do before we can officially hire you, but I don't see a problem."

The room seemed to close in on Bethany suddenly. She felt a churning sensation in her stomach, a gripping feeling in her chest. This was all wrong. She couldn't do it. She had to get back to Clearview. As quickly as she could, Bethany high-tailed it out of that man's office. She wasn't even sure what she said to him, but she must have sounded professional. He'd extended his hand and told her that he looked forward to having her on board.

178

It didn't matter. Bethany needed to get back to Clearview. Back to familiar territory. Back home. The flight home seemed longer than ever. She knew that she belonged in Clearview, and she was determined now, more than ever, to make things work. She could talk to this human resources guy later.

A wave of disappointment flooded Bethany when she looked around the airport terminal and didn't spot anyone she knew. Somehow, in the back of her mind, she'd hoped someone would have met her there. She distinctly remembered telling David and Denise the time of her return flight. Maybe she'd made a mistake. Maybe they had already resumed the lives they'd had before she'd ever arrived. She slumped over as she thought that maybe she should have accepted one of those positions in Nashville.

Then, she pulled herself up to her full height. She had to stop thinking like that. Even if her new friends *had* gone back to the way things were before she'd returned to Clearview, she still had a place here. She had a business, and she was certain that once she explained her thoughts and feelings to her friends, they'd come around and take her back in.

The first place Bethany went when she got to town was Nana's apartment, where she knew her grandmother had already returned. Mr. Michaels had personally offered to help her get settled back in, with the promise from Bethany that she'd make sure things went well for a couple of days before she moved out.

Nana sniffed the air when Bethany walked in the door. That wasn't quite the reception Bethany had expected, but she accepted it. After all, she knew that people had to guard their hearts.

After a little bit of fussing over her grandmother, Bethany looked the older woman in the eyes and said, "I'm not leaving Clearview, no matter how much you try to talk me into it."

Nana's expression went from a deep sadness to shock, then softened into a smile. "I didn't think you were stupid, Bethany. I knew you'd do the right thing."

Bethany chuckled. "It took a job offer to make me realize how much I had here. When I weighed moving to Nashville with hanging around here a while longer, I figured it would be a whole lot more fun to get in your hair a little so I could drive you nuts."

"And you're so good at it too," Nana said with a smile. "Have you spoken to David?"

"Not yet. I figured that could wait until tomorrow."

"I don't think so," Nana said, shaking her head but still smiling. "He's a basket case, that boy. I can't remember ever seeing him so worried about anything as long as I've known him."

"What do you mean, Nana?" Bethany asked, her heart pounding at the mention of David's name. "Have you talked to him today?"

Waving her hand from the wrist, Nana said, "Have I talked to him today? It seems that's all I've been doing all day. He wouldn't leave me alone about it." Mocking David's voice, Nana added, "Do you think Bethany will really move? Do you think I can talk her out of it? Why is she doing this?" Then, she went back to her own voice. "I told him that he needed to discuss his feelings with you."

The last thing Bethany needed to do was get her hopes up. "What should I do now, Nana? Call him?"

"No, no, Bethany. You have to go over there and talk to him in person. News like this should never be broken over the telephone."

Bethany was exhausted, both mentally and physically. Her emotions were raw, right on the edge of her skin. If David said something that didn't agree with what Nana had told her, she wasn't sure what she'd do. But Nana was right. She needed to go over to his house and have a long talk with him.

She quickly changed into more comfortable clothes, then left again. The drive to his house seemed to take forever, but it couldn't have been more than ten minutes. All lights were on across the front of his house. Bethany chuckled. Jonathan had a tendency to be all over the place, so she figured he'd been running around downstairs from room to room, wearing his uncle out. Fortunately, David had more energy than most adults.

She got out of the car, went up the walk, and knocked on the front door. In less than a second, the door swung open, as if he knew she was there already.

David's face lit up at the sight of her, then a split second later, it appeared that a screen had filtered his excitement as the light in his eyes faded. "Come on in," he said, stepping to the side.

She followed him inside the house, but he just stood in the hallway, waiting for her to say something. "David," she said softly, reaching out and touching his arm. He tensed. "I've decided to stay in Clearview."

It took a second for her comment to register. Then, she saw an expression of hope. "I'm sorry if my recommendation wasn't good enough to get you the job."

"Oh, it was good enough," she said with a forced smile. "In fact, I was offered the position on the spot. But I didn't take it."

"You didn't?" he asked, a full smile creeping across his lips. Then, he took her hand and pulled her toward the kitchen, the heart of this big, old, wonderful house. "Tell me all about it while I fix some tea."

Bethany told David all the details she could remember as he stood at the stove and waited for the kettle to whistle. Then, as he set the cups on the table and lowered himself into the chair, she finished by saying, "I've decided to stick around Clearview for a while, see where my bookkeeping service can go, maybe buy a house of my own."

David slowly shook his head as he lifted his cup to his lips. "You might want to hold off on buying a house."

"Why's that?" she asked. It seemed like the responsible thing to do, once she had the money for a down payment.

"I was thinking that you might want to move back into your childhood home," he said, his gaze fixed on hers. "Unless, of course, it would bother you. Then, we could sell this place and find one you would be happier with."

"What?" she said, her heart doing that flippy-flop thing again. "What are you saying, David?"

David set his cup back on the table, took her hands in his as he squirmed out of his chair and got down on one knee, never taking his eyes off hers. "I'm asking you to marry me, Bethany. I know you've been through a lot, but my love for you is growing every day I'm around you. I want to share our lives."

For the second time that day, Bethany felt dizzy. Only this time, it was from the happiness she felt in her heart. She leaned over and kissed him on the lips, then leaned back to give him her answer. "I love you too, David. Yes, I'll marry you."

"The house?" David asked, smiling with his whole face.

"We can stay right here. I'll show Jonathan how to plant a garden in the spring, and we can have people from the church over for garden parties when the flowers bloom."

"That sounds perfect, Bethany," David said as he stood and pulled Bethany to her feet. "When did you know how you felt about us?"

Bethany rocked back on her heels and thought about it for a moment. Then, she laughed. "It's been a gradual process, but I think it hit me when I saw my initials underneath the arm of the chair you made for Nana."

"I could tell she was sad about having to take the tree down, so I decided to give her the part back that seemed to mean the most to her."

Bethany hugged David, feeling wonderful that she was now free to express her feelings. His kindness was the fuel that fed the spark she'd felt when she first met him. And now, she had everything she wanted in life, and she couldn't be happier.

"Excuse me, Bethany," David said, pulling from her embrace. "I need to place a call to a very important person.

Bethany backed away, wondering who in the world he needed to call at a time like this. It was Denise. Bethany heard the squeal all the way on the other side of the kitchen. Then, he hung up and looked at Bethany. "She said to tell you congratulations and that she's very happy for us." He thought for a moment, then added, "Call your grandmother."

"Gladly," she said.

Gertie's laughter was so loud, Bethany had to hold the phone a foot from her ear. "It's about time you two came to your senses," Nana said.

Epilogue

Two years later, David and Bethany sat in the back-yard swing, enjoying the sounds of the autumn leaves as they rustled in the wind. Jonathan was digging up the last of the summer garden, showing them the bucket as he filled it with the remaining vegetables.

Bethany shifted uncomfortably, trying to find a position that didn't make her feel like a hippo. David helped her get adjusted.

"I'm glad Mary and Dallas finally got their act together, but I have to admit, I'll miss Jonathan when he leaves," Bethany said.

"They're only going to be a couple of blocks away," David said. "It's not like they're leaving town."

Bethany sighed. "I know, but I love reading to him at night." She enjoyed everything about having a child in the house, all the way down to having to prod him to do his homework.

"Just think, Bethany, it'll only be a few more weeks until we have our own child to read books to." He reached over and patted her stomach. She rested her hand on his.

Chuckling, Bethany said, "That is, if we can ever get Nana to back off long enough. I don't think I've ever seen anyone as excited about a child being born."

"Yes, she is rather exuberant, isn't she?" David agreed, adding his laughter to the sounds of the day.

"To put it mildly."

Nothing in Bethany's life before she met David could compare to what she had now. And it kept on getting better.